Garrison Tales from Tonquin

GARRISON TALES FROM TONQUIN

AN AMERICAN'S STORIES OF THE FRENCH FOREIGN

LEGION IN VIETNAM IN THE 1890s

JAMES O'NEILL

Edited, with an Introduction, by Charles Royster

LOUISIANA STATE UNIVERSITY PRESS

BATON ROUGE

PUBLISHED BY LOUISIANA STATE UNIVERSITY PRESS

Originally published in Boston by Copeland and Day, 1895.

FIRST PRINTING

DESIGNER: *Amanda McDonald Scallan*
TYPEFACE: *New Caledonia*
PRINTER AND BINDER: *Edwards Brothers, Inc.*

Library of Congress Cataloging-in-Publication Data
O'Neill, James, b. 1860.
 Garrison tales from Tonquin : an American's stories of the French
Foreign Legion in Vietnam in the 1890s / James O'Neill ; edited, with
an introduction by Charles Royster.
    p. cm.
 Originally published: Boston : Copeland and Day, 1895.
ISBN-13: 978-0-8071-3180-0 (cloth : alk. paper)
ISBN-10: 0-8071-3180-6 (cloth : alk. paper)
 1. France. Armée. Légion étrangère—Fiction. 2. Vietnam—Fiction.
I. Royster, Charles. II. Title. III. Title: Tales from Tonquin.
PS2489.O63G37 2006
813'.5—dc22

                                                    2006005859

The paper in this book meets the guidelines for permanence and
durability of the Committee on Production Guidelines for Book
Longevity of the Council on Library Resources. ∞

CONTENTS

EDITOR'S ACKNOWLEDGMENTS

My encounter with James O'Neill began during a stay at the Henry E. Huntington Library, and I wrote the biographical essay during a subsequent stay. I am grateful to Robert C. Ritchie for his hospitality. I thank the many people who helped me. These included Paul Zall, the late Martin Ridge, and especially Robert T. Smith and Patricia C. Smith.

Louisiana State University supported this project. I owe much to the assistance of my colleagues and friends William J. Cooper, Jr., Paul Paskoff, and Victor Stater.

I received documents from Sister Catherine Louise of the Society of St. Margaret, from Wayne H. Kempton of the Episcopal Diocese of New York, and from Laura Tosi of the Bronx County Historical Society. The American Antiquarian Society and the Norwood Historical Society provided photocopies of correspondence.

An editor's editor, John Easterly of Louisiana State University Press befriended James O'Neill first and last. Wayne Edmondson digitized the text for the press. Alisa Plant and Cynthia Williams guided the editor through production.

For aid, advice, and friendship, I thank James Boyden and Frank Smith.

JAMES O'NEILL
Foreign Legionnaire and Writer

The publishers Copeland and Day of Boston announced among their new books for the autumn of 1895 a volume of short stories, *Garrison Tales from Tonquin*, by James O'Neill. Its earlier working title had been *Tonquin Tales*, which survived as the running head on even-numbered pages. The word for northernmost Vietnam was usually spelled "Tonquin" in English and "Tonkin" in French. O'Neill preferred the spelling "Tong-King," now thought to be a phonetic rendering of "Dông Kinh"—that is, "capital of the East," a city where Hanoi later stood.[1] The publishers added the words "Garrison Tales" in order to market O'Neill as the Kipling of Indochina. They advertised: "The ground which Mr. O'Neill has broken for the first time is as fresh and unknown as was India before Mr. Kipling brought it home to us."[2] Beginning in 1888, Rudyard Kipling's *Plain Tales from the Hills* attracted many readers, including James O'Neill. Soon Kipling had few rivals in popularity; *The Second Jungle Book* was one of the six most widely read new books in America in December 1895.[3]

Kipling was five years younger than O'Neill. He felt empathy with British soldiers; as a newspaperman, he had seen them in India.[4] When Kipling's fiction came into vogue, O'Neill, an American, was a private in the French Foreign Legion. He, too, began to write stories of soldiers. But his opinion about European empires in Asia was very different from that of Kipling. Kipling saw their cost but said the British must persevere. For O'Neill, em-

1. Philippe Franchini, "L'or et le sang de la France," in *Tonkin 1873–1954, colonie et nation: le delta des mythes*, ed. Philippe Franchini (Paris, 1994), 13.

2. Advertisement, *The Dial* 19 (Dec. 1, 1895): 310.

3. Mark Sullivan, *Our Times: The United States, 1900–1925*, vol.1, *The Turn of the Century* (New York, 1926), 203; William Archer, *America To-day: Observations and Reflections* (New York, 1899), 132. See also Harold Orel, *The Victorian Short Story: Development and Triumph of a Literary Genre* (Cambridge, 1986), chap. 7.

4. Mark Paffard, *Kipling's Indian Fiction* (New York, 1989), chap. 3.

pires were futile, ephemeral, and destructive to the conquerors as well as to Asians. He hoped that his tales would help Americans to avoid Europeans' mistakes.

Two years old in 1895, the firm Copeland and Day lasted another four years, until its chief financial supporter, Fred Holland Day, turned from publishing to photography. He had the resources of a fortune his father had made in leather; he could pursue any enthusiasm he chose. He built the best collection in America of books and manuscripts related to John Keats. Years later, an acquaintance recalled Herbert Copeland, who was twenty-six years old when the firm began: "He was a kindly soul who tried to think he lived in Bohemia and was surrounded by a group of brilliant cognoscenti and sophisticates—American Oscar Wildes and Aubrey Beardsleys."[5] Fred Holland Day was three years older than Copeland and four years younger than O'Neill. In his teens Day admired Oscar Wilde from afar, contriving to see him during Wilde's American tour in 1882. In the 1890s Day attended concerts dressed more flamboyantly than other Bostonians, often accompanied by some exotic-looking young man drawn from one of Boston's immigrant neighborhoods. Copeland, Day, and their fellow aesthetes thought themselves to be living on a higher plane of perception and a more intense level of experience than ordinary people, above the vulgarity of American life. They numbered themselves with arbiters of refinement and art, such as George Santayana and Bernard—then Bernhard—Berenson.[6]

5. Arthur Stanwood Pier to Joe W. Kraus, Jan. 16, 1941, in Joe W. Kraus, *Messrs. Copeland & Day* (Philadelphia, 1979), 6; Ralph Adams Cram, *My Life in Architecture* (Boston, 1936), 18.

6. Estelle Jussim, *Slave to Beauty: The Eccentric Life and Controversial Career of F. Holland Day* (Boston, 1981); Verna Posever Curtis and Patricia J. Fanning, "F. Holland Day: Beauty Is Youth," in *Priceless Children, American Photographs, 1890–1925: Child Labor and the Pictorialist Ideal* (Greensboro, N.C., 2001), 33–44; James G. Nelson, *The Early Nineties: A View from the Bodley Head* (Cambridge, Mass., 1971); Douglass Shand-Tucci, *Ralph Adams Cram: Life and Architecture*, vol. 1, *Boston Bohemia, 1881–1900* (Amherst, Mass., 1995), esp. 39–45, 355–58; Mary Warner Blanchard, *Oscar Wilde's America: Counterculture in the Gilded Age* (New Haven, Conn., 1998), chap. 1.

The firm Copeland and Day was one of several similar publishing companies established by young Harvard men with their
fathers' money. They intended their books to stand apart from the
common run of American publishing, both in the quality of well-
made books and in unconventional, innovative authors. The colo-
phon of a Copeland and Day book proclaimed the founders' view
of the enterprise: a lily with the motto "sicut lilium inter spinas"—
as a lily among thorns. Copeland and Day became the American
publishers of the short-lived periodical *The Yellow Book*, which
brought Aubrey Beardsley's drawings their widest fame. The firm
issued Stephen Crane's *The Black Rider and Other Lines* several
months before O'Neill's book.[7] Although a few Copeland and Day
books sold well, the firm had a reputation as "Publishers of First
Editions"—that is, books that never went into a second printing.[8]
These volumes were beautiful, in the manner of the creations of
William Morris. Day drew his designers from among the coterie
of self-consciously aesthetic young men who gathered in Boston
to serve the cause of art. For O'Neill's book he ordered special
rice paper from Japan, and he employed a Chinese artist, Jo Hing,
to create a poster.[9]

Like other aesthetes in the 1890s, Day took an interest in
people, objects, and ideas then described as "oriental." To him
this meant primarily China and Japan, but he was also willing to
look at Indochina. The word then covered everything from Burma
to present-day Vietnam, and the region appeared in the news as
Britain and France vied for territory and influence there. The stories O'Neill submitted to Day in March 1895 and afterward dealt

7. Hamlin Garland, *Roadside Meetings* (New York, 1931), 193–200; Amy Low-
ell, "Introduction," in *The Work of Stephen Crane,* ed. Wilson Follett (New York,
1925), 6:ix; Carlin T. Kindilien, *American Poetry in the Eighteen Nineties* (Provi-
dence, R.I., 1956), 155–60.

8. Mark A. DeWolfe Howe, *A Venture in Remembrance* (Boston, 1941), 169.

9. Nancy Finlay, *Artists of the Book in Boston, 1890–1910* (Cambridge, Mass.,
1985); Eileen Boris, *Art and Labor: Ruskin, Morris, and the Craftsman Ideal in
America* (Philadelphia, 1986), chap. 3; William Dana Orcutt, *The Kingdom of Books*
(Boston, 1927), 148; *Publishers' Weekly* 48 (Nov. 2, 1895): 739; *The Critic* 24 (Nov.
2, 1895): 293.

with characters in the Red River valley of Tonkin: Vietnamese inhabitants (then called Annamites), legionnaires, and sometimes a French civilian official or missionary priest. O'Neill first sent five tales; the book grew to thirteen, and O'Neill wrote a few more that Day did not print.

Garrison Tales from Tonquin received some public notice. A leading bookstore in New York, Brentano's, stocked it. At $1.25 it was not a bargain in 1896. Advertisements listed O'Neill, with other Copeland and Day authors, in *Publishers' Weekly, The Nation, The Book Buyer, The Dial,* and *The Chap-Book.* A two-sentence summary appeared in *Publishers' Weekly.* The book was listed but not reviewed in the *Atlantic Monthly, The Critic,* and the *Chicago Tribune.* The "oriental" elements of its manufacture drew attention. Day also put out a separate limited run of thirty copies with larger pages of China paper flecked with gold, and a binding "in Oriental style laced with red cord."[10] These he offered for $3.00. Bibliophiles did not respond; of these special copies, twenty were still in stock in 1899.

O'Neill was fortunate in the thoughtfulness if not the number of reviews. True, the *Boston Journal's* critic was obtuse: "The author has a knack of picking a simple event and setting it in a simple frame as a picture of Anamese life." *Publishers' Weekly* saw "pathetic incidents of army life."[11] But reviewers in the *Hartford Courant, The Bookman,* and the *New York Times* recognized that O'Neill's stories held more than simple events and incidents. These critics wrote of "a certain mystery or melancholy," of "a sad mystic strain," and of "moving and artistic fiction of a high order." O'Neill wrote to Day: "These tales are taken from life—from my

10. Kraus, *Copeland & Day,* 120. *Garrison Tales from Tonquin* was advertised in *Publishers' Weekly* 49 (May 30, 1896): 925; *The Nation* 61 (Dec. 12, 1895): xiv; *The Book Buyer* 12 (Dec. 1895): 731; *The Dial* 19 (Dec. 1, 1895): 310; and *The Chap-Book* 4 (Dec. 1, 1895): 119. It was summarized in *Publishers' Weekly* 48 (Dec. 7, 1895): 1082; it was listed in the *Atlantic Monthly* 77 (Feb. 1896): 280; *The Critic* 24 (Nov. 30, 1895): 377; and the *Chicago Tribune,* Nov. 23, 1895.

11. Quoted in advertisement, *The Dial* 20 (March 16, 1896): 154; *Publishers' Weekly* 48 (Dec. 7, 1895): 1082.

personal experiences," and "I was confident they were good."[12] O'Neill left no record of having read any reviews. *The Bookman*'s was almost certainly written by Harry Thurston Peck, who recently had started the periodical. He was a professor of Latin at Columbia University, a man of wide-ranging interests. The notice in the *Hartford Courant* might have been written by the prolific author Charles Dudley Warner, who owned a percentage of the paper and still reviewed books in his retirement.[13] The *New York Times* critic wrote: "There is a strange, new charm in these tales, which one feels must be a true thing." Though *Garrison Tales from Tonquin* attracted some discriminating attention, it, too, was one of Copeland and Day's "first editions." It sold about fifty copies in its first nine months and another fifty-four copies in the following three years, leaving the publisher holding the bulk of the print run.

James O'Neill was born in 1860. His family lived in Bridgeport, Connecticut. He later used the home of John O'Neill—or O'Neil—as his Bridgeport address. John worked for the White Manufacturing Company, makers of fixtures for carriages and hearses. John's neighbors were carpenters, shoemakers, house painters, masons, and other skilled workers.[14] Of his youth James said: "I was much at school—more than a poor boy sh'd have been!"[15] In the 1870s James and his sister, Mary, to whom he later dedicated his book, became involved with two Anglican religious

12. Quoted in the *Hartford Courant,* Dec. 19, 1895; *The Bookman* 2 (Jan. 1896): 438; and the *New York Times,* Nov. 27, 1895; also James O'Neill to Fred Holland Day, June 1, May 2, 1895, Copeland and Day Papers, American Antiquarian Society, Worcester, Massachusetts.

13. Thomas Beer, *The Mauve Decade* (New York, 1926), 196; John Bard McNulty, *Older Than the Nation: The Story of the Hartford Courant* (Stonington, Conn., 1964), 143; Annie Adams Fields, *Charles Dudley Warner* (New York, 1904), 182.

14. *Bridgeport City Directory: 1895* (Bridgeport, Conn., 1895), 468; *American Carriage Directory: 1899* (New Haven, Conn., [1899]), 146.

15. James O'Neill to Fred Holland Day, June 1, 1895, Copeland and Day Papers, American Antiquarian Society.

orders trying to revive the spirit of the cloister in the modern church and doing good works among the poor. The Society of St. John the Evangelist—known as the Cowley Fathers—made its first move to establish an American branch in 1870, five years after Father Richard M. Benson had founded this celibate missionary order in Cowley, a suburb of Oxford. The newly ordained Father Arthur Crawshay Hall set up a community in North Bridgeport late in 1873. At about the same time, the missionary sisterhood of nurses, the Society of St. Margaret, organized a branch in Boston and accepted an invitation to take charge of that city's Children's Hospital. A scrapbook in the papers of the society records that Mary O'Neill "was one of the earliest sisters, coming to us from Bridgeport in the seventies, one of three young women who had been inspired by Father Hall's teaching to try their vocation at St. Margaret's."[16] She took the name Sister Frances.

A falling out with a local sponsor, as well as friction with the bishop, led the Cowley Fathers to abandon Bridgeport after one year and withdraw to Boston.[17] During that year or later in Boston, James O'Neill formed ties with them. At the end of the 1870s he sailed for England to spend three years in the Mission House in Cowley with Father Benson and the other priests. The University of Oxford licensed the Mission House "as 'Benson's Hall' for undergraduates who, desiring to prepare for the ministry, could not afford the ordinary college expenses." The regimen was purposely austere, with a meager diet and manual labor.[18] O'Neill did not become a student in the university, but, as a lay brother, he seems to have spent time in reading and study. In the census of

16. Scrapbook, Society of St. Margaret, Boston, Massachusetts.

17. Robert Cheney Smith, *The Cowley Fathers in America: The Early Years* (n.p., [1958]), 13–16; Shand-Tucci, *Boston Bohemia,* 187–91; George Lynde Richardson, *Arthur C. A. Hall, Third Bishop of Vermont* (Boston, 1932), 32–33.

18. Arthur C. A. Hall, "Introductory Memoir," in *Letters of Richard Meux Benson,* ed. G. Congreve and W. H. Longridge (London, 1916), 7; Peter F. Anson, *The Call of the Cloister: Religious Communities and Kindred Bodies in the Anglican Communion* (London, 1956), 80; James Nash, "The New People of East Oxford: The Suburbanisation of Cowley, 1851–91," *Oxoniensia* 63 (1998): 140.

1881 he was, at twenty-one, the youngest of the twenty-two men in the house. He later said that those three years "were not lost to me." He spent a summer in Switzerland before going back to the United States. This excursion, he later wrote, "was indirectly the cause of my return to Europe in 1887."[19] During that year he enlisted in France's Foreign Legion. In the 1880s and 1890s few Americans served in the legion. To meet one was so uncommon as to call for mention. Frederic Martyn, in a regimental office about 1890, saw an "abstract of nationalities," which set the number of American legionnaires at twenty-eight. During his time he met only two.[20]

In accounts of the Foreign Legion before the First World War, authors routinely asserted that legionnaires sooner or later regretted having enlisted. But some never looked back. A German legionnaire told an American traveler in 1894: "Future or no future, the life is one that suits me. I am now sergeant; I may be next year an officer. Last year I was fighting down in Soudan; next year I may be in Siam. We are sent to any part of the world, and do not complain. . . . I am a soldier of fortune; and, after all, are we not all at the same trade?"[21] This outlook held some attraction for O'Neill. Four years after his discharge—after he had written his tales—he still toyed with the notion of reenlisting, at the age of thirty-six.

Once in the legion, men had little choice but to say, with the German sergeant, "future or no future." They usually came to the view James Jones later found in all combat soldiers: "It is the individual soldier's final full acceptance of the fact that his name is already written down in the rolls of the already dead. . . . He

19. James O'Neill to Fred Holland Day, June 1, 1895, Copeland and Day Papers, American Antiquarian Society.

20. Georges d'Esparbès, *La Légion étrangère* (Paris, [1901]), 22; Frederic Martyn, *Life in the Legion from a Soldier's Point of View* (New York, 1911), 270–71.

21. Poultney Bigelow, "French Fighters in Africa," *Harper's New Monthly Magazine* 90 (Feb. 1895): 376–77. For an authoritative account of the legion see Douglas Porch, *The French Foreign Legion: A Complete History of the Legendary Fighting Force* (New York, 1991).

must make a compact with himself or with Fate that he is lost.
Only then can he function as he ought to function, under fire."[22]
In addition to its adventurers, soldiers from other nations, and
French recruits, the legion was also well known as a last resort of
the desperate. One of O'Neill's legionnaires is "Rotgé, a burned-
out Parisian." Pay was hardly an incentive. A private received the
equivalent of about one cent per day; the United States Army
paid twenty-five cents and the British Army about the same, a
shilling. A legion recruit received uniforms, a bed in barracks, and
standard gray army bread with two daily servings of "soupe"—usually a stew of macaroni and rice. The legion's chief attraction was
described by the German sergeant: "That is the beauty of the Foreign Legion. They ask no questions."[23] In other words, a man's
past was not held against him. Almost all O'Neill's legionnaires are
hiding something or running from something.

The two regiments of the legion had a total of about nine thousand men. During O'Neill's time a French officer wrote of them,
in a romantic vein: "Russians or Americans, Germans or Spaniards, gentlemen or vagabonds—all, in donning the blue capote,
have broken with their past existence; all have only one family:
the Legion, and one faith: their flag."[24] But this was not the full
story. At about the same time, a major in the French Army tried
to dissuade an English volunteer from enlisting in the legion, saying: "The Legion—why, you don't know what it is. Well, I will tell
you—hard work—hard knocks—hard discipline, and no thanks.
And how does it end? Your throat cut by some thieving Arab if
you have luck; if not, wounded, and then his women make sausage
meat of you. In Tonquin the same sort of thing—only worse, with
fever and sunstroke into the bargain. A bad business!"[25] O'Neill
entered the legion's Second Regiment, which had its headquarters
and training near the Algerian city of Saïda, about 120 kilometers
southeast of Oran. The First Regiment's headquarters were at Sidi

22. James Jones, *WWII: A Chronicle of Soldiering* (New York, 1976), 43.

23. Bigelow, "French Fighters," 376.

24. Frédéric Garcin, *Au Tonkin: un an chez les Muongs* (Paris, 1891), 276.

25. George Manington, *A Soldier of the Legion* (London, 1907), 10.

Bel Abbès, fifty-five kilometers south of Oran. Training lasted two months; men learned the ways of the legion—such as, a legionnaire later recalled, to sleep on a hard surface, to suffer from thirst, to march in the blazing sun and the burning sand, to hunt for something to cook, only to find nothing but rocks.[26] For more advanced training in movement and combat, the legion relied on the ability of recruits to learn from experienced men.

From time to time regimental headquarters in Algeria sent a battalion—as many as one thousand men—to Tonkin, to Dahomey, later to Madagascar, where they served with soldiers of the regular army, with the *infanterie de marine,* and with indigenous levies and recruits. In March 1890 O'Neill was one of three hundred legionnaires from his regiment crowded on board the steamship *Colombo* at Oran, sailing for Tonkin. Two years later, twenty-seven of them returned.[27] Not all the others died in Tonkin. Some men's term of enlistment ended; soldiers who survived wounds or contracted serious diseases often were sent back early. Despite the rate of loss, legionnaires volunteered for Tonkin and put their names on waiting lists. Compared to duty in Algeria or to other combat assignments, Tonkin offered novelties and comforts with, by 1890, less risk of death in battle than during the 1880s. And if Tonkin meant death, so might the legion's other destinations.

Reminders of high mortality recur in O'Neill's tales. His unpublished "Introductory" gives a sample exchange between two legionnaires reunited after their return from Tonkin:

> "Did you know such an one?"
> "Yes; he is dead."
> "And that other?"

26. Le soldat Silbermann, *Souvenirs de campagne* (Paris, 1910), 2–3, 14–15.

27. James O'Neill to Fred Holland Day, [June 1896], Fred Holland Day Papers, Norwood Historical Society, Norwood, Massachusetts; "Introductory," in James O'Neill to Fred Holland Day, June 9, 1895, Copeland and Day Papers, American Antiquarian Society; M. Adam, "Steam to Indo-China," *Sea Breezes,* n.s., 40 (Aug. 1966): 558–59.

"Dead."
"And he?"
"He too is dead."

Deaths mounted in number despite official declarations of success in pacification. O'Neill's stories take place in what he calls "that fatal country."[28] As Virginia Thompson explained fifty years later: "The Legionaries were the martyrs of the regular army, largely because they lacked influence at home."[29]

O'Neill's book, nevertheless, is not an anti-legion polemic. He did not write in order to turn his readers' thoughts in that direction. Nor do his stories offer details of atrocities inflicted on Vietnamese or describe captured legionnaires to whom "unspeakable things were done."[30] He later wrote: "We know very well that 'truth is stranger than fiction,' and so fiction should be careful not to sail too near the truth, when it becomes so 'passing strange.'"[31] In other words, fiction must not tell all that its author knows, lest his truth's strangeness make it unbelievable or unbearable. O'Neill's chief overt concern in his stories is to depict France's vain effort to conquer and govern Indochina. For most of his char-

28. "Introductory," in James O'Neill to Fred Holland Day, June 9, 1895, Copeland and Day Papers, American Antiquarian Society. See also the dedication in [Albert de Pouvourville], *Le Tonkin actuel: 1887–1890* (Paris, 1891), 5–6, 130–42; [Émile-Léopold Flourens], *Souvenirs d'Annam: 1886–1890* (Paris, 1890), vii.

29. Virginia Thompson, *French Indo-China* (New York, 1937), 75; Gilles de Gantès, "Migration to Indochina: Proof of the Popularity of Colonial Empire?" in *Promoting the Colonial Idea: Propaganda and Visions of Empire in France,* ed. Tony Chafer and Amanda Sackur (Basingstoke, 2002), 208; Nicola Cooper, *France in Indochina: Colonial Encounters* (Oxford, 2001), 126–27. See also Edward Alexander Powell, *In Barbary* (New York, 1926), 328.

30. Nguyen Thuong Hien, "Tearful Conversation over the Mulberry Fields and the Sea," in Truong Buu Lam, *Colonialism Experienced: Vietnamese Writings on Colonialism, 1900–1931* (Ann Arbor, Mich., 2000), 167–69; Paul Bourde, *De Paris au Tonkin* (Paris, 1885), 217–18; William C. Brownell, *French Traits: An Essay in Comparative Criticism* (New York, 1889), 361; Hugh Clifford, "The Legion of Strangers," *Living Age* 235 (Nov. 29, 1902): 562.

31. James O'Neill, "Maurus Jókai," *The Critic* 31 (Nov. 6, 1897): 261.

acters he conveys sympathy. Through his narratives of individuals, he tacitly appeals, as do Kipling and Crane, for compassion.[32] The *Hartford Courant*'s reviewer called O'Neill "a deep man, and one brooding upon the great problems of race and religion."[33] Six months earlier, O'Neill had written in his unpublished draft: "Our sympathies can reach to the ends of the world, unchecked by the accidents of race and religion."[34] He had no way to foresee how few readers his book would find, but this was the direction in which he wished to turn Americans.

France's intrusion in Vietnam began with missionaries. In his tale of a seemingly well-intentioned and unfortunate priest, "Père Loraine," O'Neill summarizes the pattern of that ominous overture to later French designs of conquest. Père Loraine is a Catholic missionary who arrives in Tonkin in the 1860s, when Napoleon III authorized the first military occupation of provinces in southern Vietnam, around Saigon.[35] French missionaries had been in Vietnam since the late sixteenth century, and Vietnamese officials came to regard them as agents of the French state, advance men for France's political and military incursions. A French priest had negotiated in the 1780s ties between the emperor and Louis XVI, but these fell into abeyance during the Revolution of 1789 and subsequent wars in Europe. However, the flow of missionaries

---

32. Bonamy Dobrée, *Rudyard Kipling: Realist and Fabulist* (London, 1967), 43–47; Jay Martin, *Harvests of Change: American Literature, 1865–1919* (Englewood Cliffs, N.J., 1967), 60–69; Henry Binder, "*The Red Badge of Courage* Nobody Knows," in Stephen Crane, *The Red Badge of Courage* (New York, 1982), 137–38; Stephen Crane to Nellie Crouse, Jan. 12, [1896], *The Correspondence of Stephen Crane,* ed. Stanley Wertheim and Paul Sorrentino (New York, 1988), 1:180.

33. *Hartford Courant,* Dec. 19, 1895.

34. "Introductory," in James O'Neill to Fred Holland Day, June 9, 1895, Copeland and Day Papers, American Antiquarian Society.

35. Theodore Zeldin, *France: 1848–1945* (Oxford, 1973–1977), 1:515; Joannès Tramond and André Reussner, *Éléments d'histoire maritime et coloniale contemporaine, 1815–1914* (Paris, 1924), 178–79; Hippolyte Rouhaud, *Les régions nouvelles: histoire du commerce et de la civilisation au nord de l'Océan Pacifique* (Paris, 1868), 211–12.

continued in the nineteenth century, and Vietnamese authorities grew ever more hostile.[36] Missionaries described their difficulties in the journal *Annales de la propagation de la foi* and elsewhere. Though these priests insisted to Vietnamese officials that French religious labors had no political purpose, the authorities remained unconvinced.

In O'Neill's tale, the arrival of French forces in Tonkin in 1884 and 1885 creates danger for an almost forgotten French mission-ary, who decides to help them. Invasion of Tonkin was one of the last steps toward incorporating Vietnam into the French empire under various euphemistic descriptions. This policy had critics in France; it did not attract eager support from the public, but suc-cessive governments pursued it. For a time, some thought that Vietnam might become the avenue to the supposedly vast market of China—one of the most durable illusions of Western nations' foreign policies.[37] Neither the Mekong River nor the Red River turned out to be feasible carriers of this imagined commerce. Dur-ing O'Neill's time in Tonkin the French were building a railroad northward: 101 kilometers at a cost of 20 million francs—about $4 million.[38] Such large sums expended in Vietnam by the govern-ment and its contractors brought profits to some Frenchmen but not to France. Rather than extracting great wealth from Vietnam or China, the policy was extracting money from taxpayers, then transferring it to persons directly or indirectly in the pay of the

36. Patrick J. N. Tuck, *French Catholic Missionaries and the Politics of Impe-rialism in Vietnam, 1857–1914: A Documentary Survey* (Liverpool, 1987); James Patrick Daughton, "The Civilizing Mission: Missionaries, Colonialists, and French Identity, 1885–1914" (Ph.D. diss., University of California, Berkeley, 2002), esp. chap. 1. On Catholic opposition see Alfred Perkins, "From Uncertainty to Opposi-tion: French Catholic Liberals and Imperial Expansion, 1880–1885," *Catholic His-torical Review* 82 (April 1996): 204–24.

37. David M. Pletcher, *The Diplomacy of Involvement: American Economic Expansion across the Pacific, 1784–1900* (Columbia, Mo., 2001); L. d'Anfreville de la Salle, "La conquête pacifique du Tonkin," *Revue politique et parlementaire* 24 (May 1900): 724–25; Pierre Guillen, *L'Expansion, 1881–1898* (Paris, 1984), 195–97.

38. Thompson, *French Indo-China*, 206.

French government. Every legionnaire knew Marseille. It was the port of the empire. The city's chamber of commerce urged an aggressive colonial policy upon officials in Paris, as did its colleagues in other ports.[39]

There were explanations other than the China market for the seemingly purposeless expense of trying to conquer Tonkin. Advocates of empire spoke of France's *mission civilisatrice,* an almost altruistic effort to bring modern European enlightenment to distant peoples. France would vindicate its stature and regenerate its culture by exporting improvement.[40] The empire could be progressive. In Saint-Haon-le-Châtel an inscription commemorating a native son told visitors that he had died in Indochina, "far from France, striving to win minds and hearts to her."[41] What could better represent France's message than its centennial gift to the United States? The Statue of Liberty—properly called "Liberty Enlightening [or Illuminating] the World"—was dedicated in New York Harbor in 1886. The following year the French erected a ¹⁄₁₆-scale version of this statue on a pedestal in a lake in Hanoi, presumably intending no irony.[42] The original would have been one of the last things O'Neill saw as he sailed for Europe in 1887. The replica, which he called "Liberty lighting the world," was one of the first things he saw in Hanoi in 1890. He wrote, presumably

39. Henri Brunschwig, *Mythes et réalités de l'imperialisme colonial français, 1871–1914* (Paris, 1960), 84–97, chap. 10; Raymond F. Betts, *Assimilation and Association in French Colonial Theory, 1890–1914* (New York, 1961); Stuart Michael Persell, *The French Colonial Lobby, 1889–1938* (Stanford, Calif., 1983).

40. Alice L. Conklin, *A Mission to Civilize: The Republican Idea of Empire in France and West Africa, 1895–1930* (Stanford, Calif., 1997), 1–23; Zeldin, *France,* 2:8–9, 936–37; Raoul Girardet, *L'Idée coloniale en France de 1871 à 1962* (Paris, 1972), esp. 86–90.

41. Jean Jules Jusserand, *What Me Befell: The Reminiscences of J. J. Jusserand* (Boston, 1934), 6.

42. Walter D. Gray, *Interpreting American Democracy in France: The Career of Édouard Laboulaye, 1811–1883* (Newark, Del., 1994), 128–33; Marvin Trachtenberg, *The Statue of Liberty,* rev. ed. (New York, 1986), esp. 221; Edward L. Kallop, Jr., *Images of Liberty: Models and Reductions of the Statue of Liberty, 1867–1917* (New York, 1986), 52, 66 n. 14.

xxii | JAMES O'NEILL: FOREIGN LEGIONNAIRE AND WRITER

with irony, of the reaction of Hanoi's people to French conquests in the Red River delta and to construction of a European quarter in the city: "Apparently they regard the advance of European civilisation with resignation if not with favor."[43]

European politicians, French and others, said that France must make gestures toward regaining the status of a great power in international affairs, a standing damaged by humiliating defeat at the hands of Prussia in 1871, followed by the forced cession of Alsace and Lorraine.[44] Through some inexact measurement of prestige, France would move up the scale of perceived power by using troops in Tonkin, Dahomey, Madagascar, and elsewhere, while not using them to attack Prussia. Not surprisingly, Otto von Bismarck was said to have encouraged the French to go into Tonkin.[45]

In his "Introductory" O'Neill mentions Admiral Courbet and Francis Garnier, officers who died, respectively, in June 1885—during France's attack on China in search of Chinese assent to France's claims in Tonkin—and in December 1873, while Garnier was trying, against orders, to sustain occupation of Hanoi.[46] O'Neill could also have mentioned the naval officer Henri Rivière, killed near Hanoi in May 1883 in a failed effort to overawe the Vietnamese with two hundred men. Rivière, too, defied orders. O'Neill contrasts such conspicuous deaths, much publicized in France, with the supposed profits anticipated from Tonkin after French occupation: "The profit has not yet appeared." Perhaps France, with a war as response to the civilizing mission, "may have repented of her generosity (!) and wished to retreat." But these officers' heroic ventures must be vindicated by taking Tonkin,

43. James O'Neill, "The Great Buddha," *Good Words* 35 (1894): 851.

44. Guillen, *L'Expansion*, 106–8.

45. D. W. Brogan, *The Development of Modern France, 1870–1939,* rev. ed. (New York, 1966), 1:183; Auguste Laugel, "The French Colonial Policy," *The Nation* 69 (Dec. 21, 1899): 464.

46. Cooper, *France in Indochina*, 21–22. On Courbet see also Avner Ben-Amos, *Funerals, Politics, and Memory in Modern France, 1789–1996* (Oxford, 2000), 226–27.

O'Neill says with sarcasm, lest anyone be forced to conclude that they "lost their lives for naught."[47]

During the hardest fighting, in the mid-1880s, French forces with Vietnamese auxiliaries took posts along the Red River and pressed into northern Tonkin. Parts of the armies of the Taiping rebellion in China had moved into Tonkin, organized as the Black Flags. Beginning in June 1882, Chinese government forces were also in Tonkin, in response to French incursions. Outlaw bands kidnapped and pillaged.[48] Vietnamese unwilling to collaborate with the French abandoned their villages to resist by raids and skirmishes. All these forces that encountered the French were usually well armed. Large numbers of Winchester repeating rifles had been imported into China, as were other modern weapons, while French soldiers still used single-shot Gras rifles. O'Neill probably faced fire from weapons manufactured in his hometown of Bridgeport, Connecticut.[49]

By the time O'Neill reached Tonkin, the legionnaires' war had entered the phase of fortified outposts, blockhouses, and marches in pursuit of "pirates," as the fighters were called. O'Neill broaches the idea of calling them "patriots."[50] He leaves French military operations vague in his tales, suggesting the interchange-

47. "Introductory," in James O'Neill to Fred Holland Day, June 9, 1895, Copeland and Day Papers, American Antiquarian Society.

48. Henry McAleavy, *Black Flags in Vietnam: The Story of a Chinese Intervention* (New York, 1968); Stanley F. Wright, *Hart and the Chinese Customs* (Belfast, 1950), 507–46.

49. Harold F. Williamson, *Winchester: The Gun that Won the West* (Washington, D.C., 1952), 48; Felicia Johnson Dayrup, *Arms Makers of the Connecticut Valley* (Northampton, Mass., 1948), 211; Lloyd E. Eastman, *Throne and Mandarins: China's Search for a Policy during the Sino-French Controversy, 1880–1885* (Cambridge, Mass., 1967), 85; Manington, *Soldier of the Legion*, 38, 93, 146; Ambroise Marie Robert Carteron, *Souvenirs de la campagne du Tonkin* (Paris, 1891), 159, 221; Jean Charbonneau, *L'Armée française en Indochine* (Paris, 1932), 21–24.

50. Compare Philippe Héduy, *Histoire de l'Indochine: la perle de l'empire (1624–1954)* (Paris, 1998), 379.

xxiv | JAMES O'NEILL: FOREIGN LEGIONNAIRE AND WRITER

able pointlessness of the army's campaigns. In one story soldiers are shown "wandering vaguely through marshy rice-fields"; in another they "chanced on a few pirates." Long columns—legionnaires, other French units, Vietnamese auxiliaries, and "cooly" laborers—passed abandoned villages and, even without a shot from their enemy, lost men who could not keep pace or who fell ill.[51] The French also encountered well-organized and disciplined guerrilla forces able to inflict defeats and to win the loyalty of Vietnamese officials. As the colonial administrator and diplomat, Paul Cambon, had foreseen at the end of 1885, "The complete occupation of Tonkin will be a quagmire."[52] Not until 1893 did "spontaneous resistance to the French invasion" subside; harassing attacks continued, and O'Neill had reason to write in 1895: "No, Tonquin is not yet pacified."[53] When O'Neill left in 1892, the provinces beyond the Red River delta, according to another legionnaire, "were rampant with brigandage and open revolt. Organized resistance to the new order of things existed within a few miles of Hanoi."[54]

O'Neill's tales are not stories of success in pacification of Tonkin. Nor is their sequence chronological; O'Neill was in Eu-

51. L. Bonnafont, *Trente ans de Tonkin* (Paris, [1921]), 26.

52. Paul Cambon to Mme. Cambon, Dec. 13, 1885, Paul Cambon, *Correspondance, 1870–1924*, ed. Henri Cambon (Paris, 1940–1946), 1:272.

53. "Introductory," in James O'Neill to Fred Holland Day, June 9, 1895, Copeland and Day Papers, American Antiquarian Society. See also Hy V. Luong, *Revolution in the Village* (Honolulu, 1992), 42; Henri d'Orléans, *Around Tonkin and Siam*, trans. C. B. Pitman (London, 1894), 79–85.

54. Manington, *Soldier of the Legion*, 79; Bonnafont, *Trente ans*, 40, 52. On resistance after 1890 see also Pierre Brocheux and Daniel Hémery, *Indochine: la colonisation ambiguë (1858–1954)* (Paris, 1995), 62–67; Charles Fourniau, *Annam-Tonkin, 1885–1896: lettrés et paysans vietnamiens face à la conquête coloniale* (Paris, 1989), chap. 4; J. Kim Munholland, "'Collaboration Strategy' and the French Pacification of Tonkin, 1885–1897," *Historical Journal* 24 (Sept. 1981): 629–50; compare Barnett Singer and John Langdon, *Cultured Force: Makers and Defenders of the French Colonial Empire* (Madison, Wis., 2004), 130–37; Paul Isoart, *Le phénomène national vietnamien de l'indépendance unitaire à l'indépendance fractionée* (Paris, 1961), 164; Henry Norman, *The Peoples and Politics of the Far East* (New York, 1895), 106–7.

rope when Fred Holland Day sent the final version to press in Boston. If the arrangement follows any design, the first story may suggest that what follows is "a writing in cipher, with a key which you can easily understand." And the last story, "The Pagoda," is where it belongs—at the end, a comic variation on the sad stories. It is set in the northwestern land of earlier inhabitants of Tonkin. As legionnaires march past "ruins of forgotten cities of unknown civilization," the narrator digresses to reflect upon the ancient people who "had been born, had grown old and died, and they never knew—never guessed, perhaps—that America existed." Here, most explicitly, O'Neill directs his book to Americans, though none of his characters, except the narrator, is American. This American narrator among the legionnaires realizes that uncounted generations lived out their lives in Tonkin, never wishing for anything from the Western Hemisphere or the United States.

About to sail to Europe in June 1895, O'Neill wrote to Fred Holland Day: "Were my sister not here I might never care to return."[55] As he thought of exile, O'Neill wrote stories that show the sufferings of those who abandon home, who leave their own people, who try to escape. Merely a *nom de guerre*—so common in the Foreign Legion—is ominous in an O'Neill character. In the first four tales each main figure comes to grief by trying to evade his earlier identity. Roebke appears to be a German, a veteran of some other army though new to the legion; he turns out to be—or claims to be—an Englishman; he is obsessed with dark secrets. Père Loraine, a Parisian priest, lives among the Vietnamese for twenty years; he adopts Vietnamese ways and speech but cannot cease to be a Frenchman, loyal to his *patrie.* In "Homesickness," Hugo Heilmann—his *nom de guerre*—cannot keep himself from running away: away from home, away from the legion, away from life. The first flight becomes the occasion for others. Slovatski, a Russian legionnaire, enlisted after a quarrel with the woman he wished to marry and with his father. The woman, a Jew, would

55. James O'Neill to Fred Holland Day, June 1, 1895, Copeland and Day Papers, American Antiquarian Society.

not marry him without his father's consent, and his father, apparently trying to disassociate the Slovatski family from their Jewish ancestors, refused to approve. Slovatski blames the Jews for his enlistment in the legion. Soon he is yet another legionnaire dying in Tonkin, and only at the moment of death—or perhaps only in the narrator's half-dreaming vision—is Slovatski reconciled with his beloved. The notion of flight from America that O'Neill entertained in 1895 echoed some of these voices of his fictional characters. Service in the Foreign Legion was, by definition, a rejection of earlier ties—ties O'Neill portrays as important, perhaps inescapable; rejection that, he suggests, is desperate and dangerous.

Similarly, collaboration with the French is lethal to O'Neill's Vietnamese characters—to the spirit and often to the body. In "The Cooly" a Vietnamese youth, pressed into temporary menial labor by the narrator and other soldiers, allows himself to be made a sort of pet or favorite by legionnaires in a post on the Red River. His father, a teacher, is intensely distressed, for he misses his son, and the family is not of the "cooly" or manual labor class. The narrator says of the boy: "For no obvious reason we called him Charlot." Almost certainly, O'Neill alludes to a story by Guy de Maupassant, "Aux champs," usually translated as "In the Country." In it a childless bourgeois couple go to peasant dwellings in Normandy and offer to buy a son—a boy named Charlot—to raise him as their own, with the eventual inheritance and with a pension for his parents. The parents indignantly refuse; the couple go to a nearby household, where they close a similar deal. This adopted boy prospers in the city, and Charlot, after seeing him, denounces his own parents for not having sold him. With this nickname O'Neill's legionnaires suggest that they have given their Charlot the opportunities his father's loving attachment and dignified self-respect would have denied him. The boy "came to be glad that the change had been made in his life"; he learns "La Marseillaise." Then, at random, Charlot is killed by a tiger. The legionnaires' casual patronage of him is unintentionally fatal. The schoolmaster father's vigil at the gate of the legionnaires' compound also ends in death, as he repeats his son's real, Vietnamese name: "For Mot-li,—for Mot-li!" Both Maupassant's story and O'Neill's hinge on paternal love, but in Maupassant, Charlot despises his peasant parents, while in O'Neill, Mot-li unwisely forsakes his parent and community for the blandishments of the French.

In "The Story of Youp-Youp" a Vietnamese woman, already a solitary figure among her neighbors, assists exhausted French soldiers during the initial invasion of Tonkin in force, as her fellow villagers join the resistance. The French government awards her one of the medals—"la médaille militaire," "la médaille du Tonkin," "la médaille du Mérite," and "la médaille coloniale"—given for extraordinary services.[56] In one such instance, a recent writer says, a Vietnamese official in Tonkin in the 1880s and 1890s—her great-grandfather—was so disturbed by his own collaboration that he hung his French medal in his pigsty.[57] As the rigors of French occupation grow more obvious, Youp-Youp realizes that she has aided the oppressors. Her neighbors show her that she is a betrayer of her people. Knowing of an imminent French attack on another village, she walks all night to its gate—to warn its people, O'Neill's narrator wishes to believe—but grows too weak in body to complete her purpose. The French column finds her at the village gate at dawn, and a soldier, seeing only an old woman in the way, casually bayonets her in the back. Her last gesture is to throw the military medal away from herself. Her final acts redeem her from her association with the French at the expense of her people.

Youp-Youp, unlike the boy Mot-li, is of the "cooly" class. A medal and a pension raise her status, not lower it, as Mot-li's father believes to be the consequence of Mot-li's work as a laborer. This contrast appears in the ironic title of the boy's story: "The Cooly." The legionnaires, supposing themselves to confer a benefit on their Charlot, in fact degrade him. In O'Neill's Tonkin no one is safe with the French. Their friendship is as destructive as their hostility.

56. [Albert de Pouvourville], *Deux années de lutte, 1890–1891* (Paris, 1892), 51; Henri Laumônier, *Contes et croquis tonkinois* (Hanoi, 1909), 87.

57. Duong Van Mai Elliott, *The Sacred Willow: Four Generations in the Life of a Vietnamese Family* (New York, 1999), 19. See also Nguyen Dinh-Hoa, *From the City inside the Red River: A Cultural Memoir of Mid-Century Vietnam* (Jefferson, N.C., 1999), 72–77.

O'Neill's tale "De Perier" dramatizes another form of attempted escape—addiction to opium. His epigraph is a slightly modified version of the epigraph for a story in Kipling's *Plain Tales from the Hills*, a brief narrative in which a "half-caste" describes his addiction.[58] In "De Perier" the narrator, temporarily in Hanoi, befriends the title character, whom he had known during the sea voyage, only to find that De Perier has turned to opium and that his use of it has gone beyond the casual to the constant and obsessive. The narrator fears that he, too, might have an affinity for addiction. Determined to sustain "strength and manhood," he nevertheless asks: "Was I not half envious of him, of his ability to escape the vexations of life?" Ready to cast De Perier off, the narrator finds that his empathy has grown too strong. In the climactic scene, on the march, De Perier is near death from lack of opium. The narrator procures some, but De Perier has regained "strength and manhood"; he throws the drug away, choosing death rather than "bondage." The narrator's closing letter to De Perier's mother somewhat anticipates Marlow's lie to Kurtz's Intended in Joseph Conrad's *Heart of Darkness*. But the letter is technically truthful, even if the recipient is allowed to believe that her son's enemy was Vietnamese, while the narrator knows that the enemy was opium and dependence upon a delusion of escape.

O'Neill depicts at least five of his legionnaires in behavior characteristic of a malady then called *le cafard*, though O'Neill does not use the word. Translated literally, *cafard* means cockroach. Describing a mental state, it means, roughly, a deep depression or "a bad fit of the blues."[59] Legionnaires supposedly were more susceptible to it, even uniquely afflicted. Heat, boredom, monotony, the sands of Algeria or the jungles of Tonkin—all grew ever more oppressive. Eventually, men snapped, legend says. Some turned their faces to the wall and waited for death; others burst out violently, committing verbal or physical assaults or killing themselves. In O'Neill's tales De Perier falls victim to opium; Hugo Heilmann

---

58. Rudyard Kipling, *Plain Tales from the Hills*, ed. H. R. Woudhuysen (London, 1990), 236.

59. Erwin Carlé, *In the Foreign Legion* (London, 1910), 188.

commits suicide; Corporal Richet in "Le Buif" loses his reason; Roebke falls into a lassitude ended by "a pirate's bullet," true to his "premonition" that transfer to Tonkin would mean his death; the narrator summarizes Slovatski's state of mind even before introducing him: "What was the use?"

O'Neill's narrator several times describes his own measures to ward off *le cafard*. He carries books on the march and reads about faraway or imaginary peoples in the works of Robert Louis Stevenson or in Camille Flammarion's *La pluralité des mondes habités;* on an "unspeakably wearisome" march he detaches his mind from the present and lives in the past; he studies the Vietnamese. Except with Corporal Richet, the narrator urges his methods on gloomy, despondent legionnaires, uniformly without success.

An Englishman who served in the Foreign Legion at the same time as O'Neill cast doubt on the common assertion that life in the legion drove men mad or afflicted them with this peculiar malady. Legionnaires, he suggested, brought their disturbed minds and depressed spirits into the legion when they enlisted. Hardly anyone except eccentric or unbalanced men would volunteer for the legion. He estimated that instances of *le cafard* ended in "tragedy" rather than in "an ordinary drunken quarrel or an extraordinary drunken spree" one time out of a hundred.[60] O'Neill's narrator gravitates toward that one. He several times mentions his "misery"; he says "alas!" that he must continue to live. Asked whether his life has no thunder, he answers with a glance: "I smiled somewhat grimly at Pho-Xa, and he understood." As he establishes that he, too, faces melancholy and a wish for death, he also shows how he endures, and he tries to get similarly burdened men to emulate him. To Hugo Heilmann, the homesick runaway, he commends the case of the cuckold in Molière's play, *George Dandin.* One could at least draw some laughter out of "bearing the results of our foolishness." But the end of Molière's comedy leaves open a possible later outcome like Hugo Heilmann's offstage fate—de-

60. Martyn, *Life in the Legion,* chap. 24. See also Ellis Ashmead-Bartlett, *The Passing of the Shereefian Empire* (1910; reprint, Westport, Conn., 1970), 116–19. For the typical view see Carlé, *In the Foreign Legion,* 183–90.

xxx | JAMES O'NEILL: FOREIGN LEGIONNAIRE AND WRITER

spair and suicide. The narrator's efforts to save legionnaires from
le cafard fail.[61]

Among O'Neill's recurrent concerns, he saved an unusual
intensity for missionary endeavor. In his stories, even apparent
conversions to Christianity in Tonkin are illusory or superficial.
Missionaries, he thought, try to change "the eternal nature of
things"—that is, in Vietnam, Buddhism. To stress the uselessness
of Père Loraine's many years of missionary labor, O'Neill seems
to interrupt his own narrator with an impatient outburst: "Think!
With fire and sword the Spaniards labored for three hundred years
to put down idolatry in Mexico, planting Christianity in its stead,
yet when an idol was unearthed there a few years ago, it was seen
that some one had come in the night and crowned it with flowers."
Such an incident at Mexico's National Museum was mentioned in
a travel book by Fanny Chambers Gooch in 1887. Newspapers of
the 1890s reported discoveries of large Aztec sculptures buried
long ago by Spaniards. In some of these accounts Indians "prayed
publicly" to "Aztec idols."[62] O'Neill depicts Christianity in Vietnam
as an impermanent, unmeaning veneer. And, evoking Mexico, he
links missionaries with fire and sword.

Pho-Xa, the eighteen-year-old Vietnamese teacher in "The
Worst of the Bargain," once had "fallen into the hands of some
French missionaries," who tried to turn him into a Christian
named Paul. Under pressure from his father and brother, who
are "with the pirates," Pho-Xa abandons Catholicism and returns
to Buddhism. He can teach children French only through a tacit
bargain with the French, whose civilization the Vietnamese must
study, he believes. His classroom follows the forms of Christian-

61. For other accounts of *le cafard* see, among many: Georges, comte de Vil-
lebois-Mareuil, "La Légion étrangère," *Revue des deux mondes,* ser. 10, 134 (April
1896): 871; Georges Gorée, *Les amitiés sahariennes du Père de Foucauld* (Paris,
1946), 1:75; d'Esparbès, *Légion étrangère,* 59–76; Philippe Franchini, *Les guerres
d'Indochine* (Paris, 1988), 1:112.

62. Fanny Chambers Gooch [Iglehart], *Face to Face with the Mexicans* (New
York, 1887), 243; *New York Times,* April 27, 1893, Oct. 30, 1892, Feb. 19, 1894;
Thomas A. Janvier, *Legends of the City of Mexico* (New York, 1910), 163; Anita
Brenner, *Idols behind Altars* (New York, 1929), chap. 6.

ity. In his private chamber of the school, however, he maintains a shrine to the Buddha. O'Neill's narrator warns him not to lead this double life of divided loyalties, but Pho-Xa perseveres. Then his brother, the "pirate," who had said that Pho-Xa ought to be dead rather than live as a Frenchman and a Christian, makes his own bargain with the French. Taken prisoner by soldiers who are about to execute him, he offers to lead them to the stronghold of the resistance in the mountains. He betrays his comrades. In return, the French spare his life, and he is released. Pho-Xa calls him "a traitor"; the brother calls Pho-Xa an apostate. Seeing Pho-Xa's schoolroom, with its Catholic symbols, the brother grows enraged and kills Pho-Xa on the spot. But, upon finding the Buddhist shrine in the private chamber, the brother, presumably overcome with remorse for his hasty murder and his own complicity with the French, falls dead, perhaps a suicide. In a touch worthy of the stage in O'Neill's day, the bodies are discovered by Pho-Xa's schoolchildren, for whose sake he made his bargain. Thus, both brothers get the worst of their bargains with the French, and the missionaries claim more victims.

O'Neill's narrator hardly stops short of ridicule for the title character of "Père Loraine." The next-to-last paragraph hints that the priest, despite his outward sacrifices in Vietnam, has been self-absorbed. Loraine would have spent his career more appropriately in Paris, among the admiring ladies who thronged to hear him preach at Saint-Sulpice. He lived the wrong story. He ought to have been a character in a Massenet opera, not a martyr to empire. O'Neill emphasizes the extent to which Vietnamese people acquainted with Père Loraine regard him as a strange foreigner, even after he has spent twenty years among them. Killings of missionaries and Vietnamese Catholics in the violence of 1882–1885 took on attributes of a popular uprising. O'Neill's story dramatizes Père Loraine's isolation from the people, making "his flock" his executioners.[63] By the time French forces invade Tonkin, Père

63. Truong Buu Lam, *Patterns of Vietnamese Response to Foreign Intervention: 1858–1900* (New Haven, Conn., 1967), 14; Daughton, "Civilizing Mission," 70–79; Léon-Xavier Girod, *Souvenirs franco-tonkinois, 1879–1886* (Paris, [1903]), 146–54.

Loraine's assistance to the soldiers plausibly looks to the Vietnamese as if he had planned it for twenty years. The tale points toward the conclusion that a missionary—even one who has lived among the populace, imagining himself to be saving souls—is inevitably an agent of imperial conquest.

Missionaries are again absurd, somewhat sinister figures in "A Dream." The narrator's dream takes him to what appears to be a temple of the essence of true religion. In its courtyard "six Roman cardinals" sleep under the eyes of the temple priests. Having preached together in an effort to convert these "heathen priests," the missionaries grew tired "after their ineffectual exertion." One cardinal wakes and tries in vain to wave the dreamer back, to divert him from the inner temple.

The dreamer has come upon this temple through an experience of fear. Before he reaches the temple, he feels himself to be on a barren seashore depicted in a painting by Jean-Léon Gérôme. There, an agitated lion walks alone near the edge of the Gulf of Aqaba. Gérôme called this painting "Quaerens Quem Devoret"—"seeking the one whom he would devour." While at work, the artist found that he first made the sky "too dark"; the scene still looked ominous when he finished it. A photogravure reproduction appeared in Fanny Field Hering's book on Gérôme, published in 1892.[64] O'Neill's dream narrator fears the lion—fears even seeing it—then grows preoccupied with a formerly distant cliff in the background; it suddenly looms nearer and nearer. Accompanied by a companion identified only as "you," he runs toward the cliff and finds that it is a great stone temple.

Briefly in "The Worst of the Bargain" and more fully in "A Dream," O'Neill raises the prospect, much discussed in his time, of a syncretic expression of the spirit of religious yearning.[65] The rites

64. The painting, now lost, was photographed. See Gerald M. Ackerman, *The Life and Work of Jean-Léon Gérôme* (London, 1986), 133 and No. 362; Fanny Field Hering, "Gérôme," *Century Magazine* 37 (Feb. 1889): 495.

65. Thomas A. Tweed, *The American Encounter with Buddhism, 1844–1912: Victorian Culture and the Limits of Dissent* (Bloomington, Ind., 1992), 115–21; Jean Pierrot, *The Decadent Imagination, 1880–1900,* trans. Derek Coltman (Chicago, 1981), 55–60; Lawrence W. Chisolm, *Fenollosa: The Far East and American Culture* (New Haven, Conn., 1963), chap. 10.

and figures in the dream's temple suggest several religions and yet no one of them alone; in the gaze of a temple priest the dreamer sees infinite sympathy and "nothing but the purest, tenderest love." The narrator first falls asleep, then dreams, and afterward wakes with his head on the Buddha's left foot—a statue in a pagoda used as a camp by the legionnaires. O'Neill often conveys his sympathy with Buddhism as he understands it. Several times he sets up contrasts between the serene Buddha, who has attained nirvana, and the restless, acquisitive, petty energy of Europeans. These imply censure of Christian churches, if not of Christianity. For O'Neill, their evangelism is impertinent, ultimately mischievous.

The epigraph of "A Dream" hints that the tale is a parable. O'Neill chooses the smoother, more irenic account of Jesus's use of parables given in the Gospel of Matthew, suggesting that parables can teach, rather than the version in Mark, which seems to say that parables conceal truths from the uninitiated.[66] In the story the narrator is frightened and anxious as he dreams, but he associates the pagoda and the Buddha with calm and peace, even after legionnaires' "desecration" of the sacred site.

O'Neill wrote in his essay on the Great Buddha statue in Hanoi: "It seemed somehow as if this image would speak to me if only I could hear and understand; such was my impression . . . in the *ensemble* there was a strange dignity—a placid calmness, and I thought: 'Surely one who had found *Nirvana* would look like that, when all earthly hopes, and fears, and longings, and strivings were over; when all human passions had passed away, such would be the expression in the face.'"[67] This description, in effect, asks: to people with such an image always before them in the mind's eye, what could missionaries bring? In "A Dream" the dreamer first reacts to waking from his anxiety in the night by turning thoughtful. Then he kisses the Buddha's foot and sleeps "in peace," still surrounded by soldiers. That which can bring peace under these circumstances, the story suggests, is worth seeking. Ultimately, a parable tells a truth people comprehend because they already know it.

66. Matthew xiii:34; Mark iv:9–13; Frank Kermode, *The Genesis of Secrecy: On the Interpretations of Narrative* (London, 1979), 28–32.

67. O'Neill, "Great Buddha."

The last story, "The Pagoda," could stand alone, but it carries more force at the end of these thirteen tales. It exploits and upsets expectations established by earlier stories. Nine of those twelve end in death—by combat, fever, murder, suicide, decapitation, tiger attack, bayonet in the back, and, apparently, grief. A tenth ends in madness. What first-time reader would expect the thirteenth story to be a funny satire?

The narrator uncharacteristically gives a date for the legionnaires' march that opens the tale: January 1890. O'Neill may have wished to set the episode in a time when he had not yet arrived in Tonkin. However, he probably drew this tale, as he did others, from his own experience, which apparently occurred in 1891.[68] He starts the story in the widest perspective—the realm of the ancient peoples who dominated the region in the fifteenth century—amid the ruins of lost civilizations.[69] The legionnaire with the greatest knowledge of antiquity, Descuret, has studied Egypt; he knows and cares nothing about the Lê dynasty in Vietnam, which lasted until the eighteenth century. These ruins mock the Europeans, indifferent to their conquests. Even the landscape seems hostile. A rigorous but fruitless march across a mysterious, threatening countryside leads to a village newly abandoned by its inhabitants, a common reaction to the approach of the French. The story narrows to this village, a pagoda, and the legionnaires' camp.

In the village the narrator and another legionnaire find chickens, fresh eggs, liquor, and many carefully preserved books—"Chinese books which no one could read." With this dismissal, Chinese civilization gets the same treatment as the Lê dynasty. Back at camp, after food, drink, and an hour's sleep, the narrator wishes to explore a pagoda he saw near the village. Descuret, the Egyptologist, wishes to find more liquor. The story soon narrows to the pagoda.

In the village with the narrator, Descuret quickly kills a chicken

68. See [Pouvourville], *Deux années*, 163–65; Emmanuel Chabrol, *Opérations militaires au Tonkin* (Paris, 1896), 52; Louis-Félix-Edmond Rouyer, *Histoire militaire et politique de l'Annam et du Tonkin depuis 1799* (Paris, [1906]), 151–54.

69. Albert de Pouvourville, *L'Art indochinois* (Paris, 1894), 213.

and starts to pluck its feathers. The narrator works to overcome Descuret's superstitious reluctance in order to persuade him to explore the pagoda. They scale a wall and enter. For the next six pages, beginning with "furious griffins with porcelain eyeballs, glittering fearfully," O'Neill makes the pagoda more and more threatening in the minds of the legionnaires. Its images, masks, and paraphernalia resemble in part those of the Yao, who are numerous in southern China and northern Tonkin.[70] The two legionnaires enter the pagoda with the "innocent intention" of stealing some "portable objects of art . . . in the face of all the gods." Instead, the works of art frighten the narrator, as Descuret continues to prowl. But the pagoda also has done its work on Descuret's mind. As he gropes amid the contents of a coffin-shaped box in search of a small bronze Buddha, he suddenly panics. The narrator uses lines from Robert Browning's "Paracelsus," evoking the odor of an Egyptian mummy's shroud,[71] to trigger the fright, yet to recall that Descuret the Egyptologist ought not to be scared by anything he finds in the box, whether a corpse or regalia for religious ceremonies. Even so, the two legionnaires run screaming from the pagoda. Back in camp, Descuret says that a long yellow hand clutched at him. He refuses to accompany the narrator back to the pagoda after they realize that they forgot their rifles, left at its gate. But as the narrator prepares to return, Descuret, still shaken by fear, has the presence of mind to tell him to pick up the half-plucked chicken in the village. There the French conqueror of Tonkin stands revealed: lost amid ruins of ancient civilizations, frightened to a state of panic in an abandoned Buddhist place of worship, disarmed by an empty pagoda, yet clinging to a bit of plunder.

70. Jess G. Pourret, *The Yao: The Mien and Mun Yao in China, Vietnam, Laos and Thailand* (Chicago, 2002); Jean Michaud, "The Montagnards and the State in Northern Vietnam from 1802 to 1975: A Historical Overview," *Ethnohistory* 47 (2000): 333–49. See also Louis Bezacier, *L'Art vietnamien* (Paris, 1955), 124–29, 141–42, 146–51, 158–59.

71. *Paracelsus,* Part 4, lines 198–200, *The Poetical Works of Robert Browning,* ed. Ian Jack and Margaret Smith (Oxford, 1983), 1:378–81.

O'Neill or any legionnaire in Tonkin knew that pagodas usually fared ill at the hands of French "pacification"; they were routinely used as campsites, incorporated into fortifications, vandalized, and marked with soldiers' graffiti. A British author later wrote: "It is not a good way to win over an essentially religious people by quartering troops and horses in their pagodas."[72] Yet the possibility of Europeans' encountering a pagoda in a respectful spirit of inquiry retained appeal, as in a sketch, "La Pagode," published by a French officer in Hanoi in 1889. A visit became a discussion of comparative religion.[73] A pagoda, like other religious sites, can affect even a skeptical or cynical mind. In O'Neill's tale his narrator is, at first, curious, then a half-hearted looter; Descuret is a looter. These legionnaires have seen many pagodas. Yet O'Neill makes this one different. With a series of small dislocations, he separates the pagoda from the village, the legionnaires from their unit, the legionnaires from the village, and the pagoda from its surroundings. At first, Descuret says: "It's the same old story that we've seen a hundred times." This thought does not reassure him for long. Perhaps because they recall similar images from a hundred times before, the legionnaires find those in the isolated pagoda growing more ominous. The narrator is soon terrified—fear that reaches a climax as he sees, among the paraphernalia, a carved face "like a hideous Japanese mask"; it "leered at me in a mad, mocking way, ghastly and horrible." This "hideous" image, for the narrator, and the mysterious hand in the box, for Descuret, become the revenge of a hundred pagodas on the two legionnaires, who have more active imaginations than they supposed.

In none of the tales does O'Neill's narrator play a bigger part than in "Eckermann and Tannemeyer." New recruits in the legion were routinely cautioned to mind their own business. The narrator ignores this advice with his fellow soldiers Eckermann and Tannemeyer. He soon finds that he has intruded upon "a passion

72. Stephen H. Roberts, *History of French Colonial Policy, 1870–1925* (London, 1929), 2:441.

73. L. Yann [Lieutenant Lassalle], *Croquis tonkinois* (Hanoi, 1889), 67–76.

of love, despair, and anguish." Is it a story of homosexuality in the legion, rendered in soft focus out of regard for taboos of the time? In *The French Foreign Legion,* Douglas Porch includes a list of colorful characters in the late nineteenth-century legion, among them "two Germans who were inseparable."[74] O'Neill's two German legionnaires fit this description by the end of their story, but not, apparently, at its start.

From the first, on board the *Colombo* en route to Tonkin, Eckermann and Tannemeyer, quartered not far apart, conspicuously avoid each other, though they are from the same city in Bavaria. The narrator, a busybody, contrives ways to bring them together or to make them aware of their similarities and sympathies. These efforts produce marks of agitation and strong emotion: Tannemeyer's "face grew white"; Eckermann was "pale and nervous." Near the end of the story, at the prospect of news of Tannemeyer, Eckermann's "face turned pale." By this point, their attachment has become common knowledge; no one cares much. The two men's continued agitation does not arise from concerns of secrecy or exposure. Through a somewhat obtuse narrator—one in whom Eckermann is unwilling to confide—O'Neill concerns himself not directly with the story of the legionnaires' love but with the story of its being thwarted: first, seemingly, by them; then by the legion's separate postings. The narrator insists that "never a word of friendship or affection had passed" between the two before their dramatic public embrace, a fraught farewell where, among the other men, "no one thought much of separation." After new assignments part them, both feign good cheer, but without conviction. The narrator finds that both are aesthetically perceptive and artistically expressive. These two German legionnaires manifest the keener sensibility then associated with the newly named phenomenon: the homosexual. They are "two Germans who were inseparable." O'Neill's obtuse narrator, both by talking to them when he ought not to talk and by not talking when he ought to talk, reveals, with seeming inadvertence until the last pages, the

74. Porch, *French Foreign Legion,* 176. See also Robert Aldrich, *Colonialism and Homosexuality* (London, 2003), esp. chap. 2.

strength of their attachment and the grief—a word he uses four times—that attends its obstruction.

The last part of the story, after their separation, is one-third of the whole. The narrator seems to be the only person who pays much attention to Eckermann and Tannemeyer. O'Neill introduces comic relief with the arrival of the governor general of Indochina. Jean-Louis de Lanessan made a tour of inspection in the summer of 1891. His appointment to his new post had been announced in Paris on April 21, 1891. Hoping that the French could govern through the established elites in Tonkin and elsewhere, he had written of "a colony of relatively advanced civilization." Its people could be "our partners in the work of civilization and progress."[75] Military men did not talk this way. O'Neill's narrator mentions soldiers' distaste for serving under a civilian in Tonkin, rather than a general. Just when Eckermann and Tannemeyer are parted, O'Neill reminds readers of the war that seems far from the two legionnaires' thoughts. In Paris a veteran of Tonkin expressed a soldier's view of the appointment of de Lanessan. He said on April 30: "Do you suppose that they'll send you civilians to govern the colony, or some men of science who imagine that all men are brothers. This isn't what is necessary in the colony; in interacting with brutes it is necessary to be brutal. If I had been named governor for only one month, I would have exterminated this entire Tonkinese world."[76] This bloodthirsty veteran states the most extreme case of those who deplored giving command of an unruly colony to a civilian who imagines that all men are brothers. The governor's tour of Tonkin provides an occasion for the narrator to go up the Red River to Yen-Bay, where he sees Eckermann. Against this backdrop of dispute over imperial policy, the two German legionnaires play out their stories.

75. Jean-Louis de Lanessan, *L'Expansion coloniale de la France* (Paris, 1886), 542; Fourniau, *Annam-Tonkin,* 185–97; V. G. Kiernan, *The Lords of Human Kind: Black Man, Yellow Man, and White Man in the Age of Empire* (Boston, 1969), 95.

76. Entry of April 30, 1891, in Wilfred Scawen Blunt, *My Diaries: Being a Personal Narrative of Events, 1888–1914,* 3d ed. (New York, 1923), 1:51. See also Jean Chesneaux, "Stages in the Development of the Vietnam National Movement 1862–1940," *Past and Present* 7 (April 1955): 66; Fourniau, *Annam-Tonkin,* 197–207.

In the time the narrator takes to continue upriver, then return to Yen-Bay, Eckermann shoots himself through the heart. Bearing this news downriver to Thanh-Ba, the narrator witnesses Tannemeyer's reaction—he shoots himself with a pistol. The narrator closes: "The next instant Tannemeyer lay dead in my arms." The descriptions of both legionnaires in their respective posts shortly before their deaths recount their efforts to distract themselves with ordinary affairs and local matters of interest. False cheer and strained enthusiasm show, in the futility of such gestures, the men's unbearable isolation. They have tried the usual expedients and found them inadequate. The narrator is reduced to a hope that Tannemeyer will already have heard of Eckermann's suicide from someone else. But Tannemeyer sees the news in the narrator's face. At the end, Tannemeyer is gazing "far off into eternity," and no one in Tonkin—or anywhere else—can help him.

The place names in Tonkin mentioned in these tales were real places, chiefly villages near French garrisons up the Red River, where legionnaires of the Second Regiment were stationed. First Regiment legionnaires went to the region nearer China in the northeast. O'Neill refers to Red River posts accurately and often, contributing to the impression or illusion of an eyewitness narrative by a trustworthy source.

Yen-Luong lies about 120 kilometers—by air, not by river—northwest of Hanoi; it figures in several stories as the narrator's assigned post. "The Cooly" and "Le Buif" take place there. Nearby Ka-Dinh—or Ca-Dinh—was the site of skirmishes with a force under the guerrilla leader De-Tham in the autumn of 1891.[77] It appears in O'Neill's tales as the direction from which Roebke is returning when killed by "a pirate's bullet" and as the objective of a painful march at the start of "Le Buif." Than-Ba—or Thanh-Ba, as it appears in the histories—is about thirty kilometers downstream from Yen-Luong. Tannemeyer is assigned to this post. Thanh-Ba is also the site of the work of the Vietnamese teacher Pho-Xa at his nominally Christian school in "The Worst of the Bargain." As in O'Neill's account of Pho-Xa's guerrilla brother, the real com-

77. *Histoire militaire de l'Indochine* (Hanoi-Haiphong, 1930), 2:43.

mandant at Thanh-Ba, Lieutenant Crouzillard, was marching in pursuit of a pirate leader in November 1891 and January 1892.[78] Ngoï-Lao, about halfway between Yen-Luong and Thanh-Ba, is the setting for "The Story of Youp-Youp." O'Neill's narrator appears as one who passes along a version of events he heard years after Youp-Youp's death. If O'Neill's tales had won American readers, few could have been expected to differentiate these Vietnamese place names from one another by their locations. Yet most of the stories strive for continuity among the tales, based partly upon fixed locales.

Early in the story "Slovatski" the title character says of the Red River posts: "I get these outlandish places mixed up." This attitude is a warning that Slovatski is in trouble. The narrator quickly instructs him about the differences. Yen-Luong would have been a better posting than Traï-Hut, where they are, and Kam-Khe—or Cam-Khé—would have been better than Yen-Luong. Traï-Hut, according to the narrator, is "one of the worst posts on the river." It lies only ninety kilometers from China by the Red River route. Its real garrison fought many engagements with "bandits" late in 1891 and early in 1892.[79] O'Neill's narrator says of the garrison in the story: "If we spent two nights a week in bed we were fortunate." Almost mockingly, place names of the Red River posts recur in Slovatski's life in Tonkin, twelve times in twelve pages, until the end, when the feverish Slovatski, being brought downriver, dies in a Chinese junk tied up for the night at Ngoi-Thie—or Ngoï-Tié.[80] To perceive this touch of irony a reader must know, without the narrator's aid, that Ngoï-Tié lies a short distance upriver from the junk's destination, the infirmary at Yen-Bay. The difference between these two posts for Slovatski is foreshadowed on the story's first page: the sick are "sure of a rest,—at the hospital or in the cemetery." Slovatski's emotional torments, which distracted him from his surroundings in Tonkin, have been framed

78. Luong, *Revolution in the Village,* 40; *Histoire militaire de l'Indochine,* 2:43–44.

79. Bonnafont, *Trente ans,* 40–41; *Histoire militaire de l'Indochine,* 2:34–36.

80. For Ngoï-Tié see Chabrol, *Opérations militaires,* 141 map.

by a trip up the river and a trip partway back down, but not quite far enough. Of course, Yen-Bay does not guarantee health and safety to troubled legionnaires. Though it is "a very fine post . . . quite the best on the river," with large brick barracks "as good as any in Algeria," its amenities do not reconcile Eckermann to life without Tannemeyer. His body is buried the morning after his suicide, presumably "on a hill, back of Yen-Bay," not far from where the mysterious Roebke is buried after he is shot by "pirates"—one more casualty, like Slovatski, in O'Neill's tightly knit society of Red River legionnaires, all of whom yet remain strangely alone.

O'Neill's earlier essay, "The Great Buddha," ostensibly described a large bronze effigy of the seated Buddha in a pagoda in Hanoi.[81] This account unfolded into a study of a lonely old man who found a purpose for his life: he appointed himself the statue's guardian and guide, living on alms from visitors. The old man was Nam-Si, and his greatest triumph, he supposed, was to prevent the French from taking the statue for display at the Paris Exposition of 1889, best known for the Eiffel Tower.

The exposition opened on May 5, 1889. Within six months 30 million people had visited it. "From the very first the Exposition was pronounced *chic.*" The Great Buddha of Hanoi was not wrested from its pagoda and its keeper to decorate the festivities in Paris, but Tonkin had a part to play in demonstrating to Europe the success of the French empire. The streets of the exposition were lined with facsimiles and artifacts from many countries and provinces. Along the Esplanade des Invalides stood the pagodas and palaces that represented France's Far Eastern world. Tonkinese auxiliary infantrymen lit lanterns in the evenings for performances by Annamese actors; "Tonkinese bonzes held a service in the pagoda, where the fruits of the Celestial Empire are sacrificed in great masses to golden Buddhas."[82] Journalists

81. See also Charles-Édouard Hocquard, *Une campagne au Tonkin* (Paris, 1892), 190.

82. Richard Kaufmann, *Paris of To-day*, trans. Olga Flinch (New York, 1891), 273–74, 293, 263.

published *L'Avenir du Tonkin illustré,* "an illustrated revue of the colonial Exposition that greatly contributed to making the new French conquest better known."[83] The exhibits, indigenous arts, and scale-model reconstructions were meant to demonstrate, two German historians later wrote, "that every nation is offering up its gifts on the altar of French civilization."[84]

Perhaps French officials never had seriously entertained the notion of moving the large statue of Buddha from Hanoi, but in Nam-Si's account he had agitated forcefully on its behalf. He protested to Vietnamese dignitaries: "What then? The French, not satisfied with having taken the country, must also try to take away its gods. Oh, but no! that should not be." Thus he had saved the statue, his chief joy. A French traveler discerned the importance of the Great Buddha to the people's pride. He wrote of this and other pagodas in Hanoi: "A feeling of patriotic gratitude attracts the native in these temples, in which hovers, hallowed and glorified by time, the memory of heroes who delivered the fatherland from danger."[85] Both this traveler and O'Neill described the popularity of the pagoda and the Great Buddha, "which pilgrims and tourists come so far to see, to pray to, or to wonder at." The pagoda of the Great Buddha figured regularly in nineteenth-century French descriptions of Hanoi. O'Neill did not mention—he might not have known—that the French administration's budget for assistance to Buddhist monuments and ceremonies paid for repairs to the pagoda.[86]

A portrait of Nam-Si, or of an old man resembling O'Neill's de-

83. Claude Bourrin, *Le vieux Tonkin: 1884–1889* (Saigon, 1935), 177; Flourens, *Souvenirs d'Annam,* chap. 21; Lynn E. Palermo, "Identity under Construction: Representing the Colonies at the Paris *Exposition Universelle* of 1889," in *The Color of Liberty: Histories of Race in France,* ed. Sue Peabody and Tyler Stovall (Durham, N.C., 2003), 285–301.

84. E. R. Curtius and A. Bergstraesser, *Frankreich* (Stuttgart, 1930), 1:18, quoted in H. L. Wesseling, *Soldier and Warrior: French Attitudes toward the Army and War on the Eve of the First World War,* trans. Arnold J. Pomerans (Westport, Conn., 2000), 55.

85. Jean de Cardaillac, *Au Tonkin: impressions et souvenirs* (Paris, 1910), 54.

86. Léon-Xavier Girod, *Dix ans de Haut-Tonkin* (Tours, [1899]), 235.

scription of Nam-Si, appeared in Émile Duboc's *Trente-cinq mois de campagne en Chine, au Tonkin.*[87] O'Neill narrated a growing acquaintance with Nam-Si: his cramped lodgings, his elegant ceramic teapot and cups, for which he could afford only bad tea, and especially his private singing in praise of the Buddha: "O Buddha, whom I now salute in humility, thou knowest that I love thee and that from the eyes of strangers who ignore thy greatness, and smile scornfully on thy servants, I have kept and guarded thine image, so sublimely majestic." Upon Nam-Si's death, O'Neill imagined that the faithful guardian's "essence has now passed into another form, and, because of his past virtues, into a higher being." Nam-Si had found with the statue and its pagoda the home, the fixed place and purpose, that O'Neill's legionnaires lack. O'Neill never returned to the pagoda in Hanoi after he learned of Nam-Si's death. He took less interest in the statue than in the old man's devotion.

The title word of the tale "Le Buif" was French military slang for "shoemaker." The epigraph is a misremembered version of a line from Pliny the Elder: "Ne supra crepidam sutor iudicaret."[88] It can be translated: "Let a cobbler not judge beyond a sandal." The customary English proverb runs: "Let the cobbler stick to his last"—which the story's closing sentence echoes. The character who endures the sobriquet "Le Buif" makes the mistake of accepting promotion to the rank of corporal. O'Neill, by choice, remained a private throughout his five years in the legion. Corporal was a difficult position, with responsibility for command of privates and for accounts of their supplies. Officers and sergeants blamed corporals for anything wrong in the ranks, but privates respected only a competent corporal. Owing to the legion's death rate, promotion was not hard to win. Hence, the rank of corporal did not always go to the able or the deserving. O'Neill's narrator does not mention the legion's tradition of "the regimental 'cor-

87. Émile Duboc, *Trente-cinq mois de campagne en Chine, au Tonkin* (Paris, [1898?]), 50.

88. Albert Barrère, *Argot and Slang: A New French and English Dictionary,* rev. ed. (London, 1889), 58; Caius Plinius Secundus, *Historia Naturalis,* II, xxxv, 85.

poral shoemaker.'"[89] Such a role would suit Richet, the cobbler known as "Le Buif," but he is too obtuse and self-important to admit his incompetence. And, perhaps, he is desperate to end the ridicule summarized in his nickname.

Trying to sustain his new rank, Richet goes on the march more often; he marches even while ill. Meanwhile, he is victimized by the sinister Sergeant Dreck, who steals the supplies of Richet's men with impunity, since Richet does not know how to prevent him. At last, these strains reach a crisis. On an especially hot day, Richet suffers brain damage. He becomes a "jabbering, gibbering idiot." O'Neill's narrator recalls his own precautions in the heat: "I put wet napkins on my head and crept away to a dark place." Richet had tried to enter the infirmary but had been rejected. In his illness he raves about his rise to ever higher rank. O'Neill translates the word *adjudant* as "adjutant," but the English word usually means a staff officer. In the French Army an *adjudant* ranked above the most senior sergeants and wielded much power over enlisted men. Consequently, Corporal Richet's loud cry—"I'll soon be an adjutant too, ha, ha!"—is the climax of his madness. The long period of being demeaned and ridiculed as an oaf and a simpleton, even by privates in the Foreign Legion, has come to a final outburst of delusional escape from being "Le Buif." Unhappily, this form of escape, O'Neill concludes, is worse than Richet's former condition.

O'Neill set himself a difficult task in the brief tale "A Spiritual Combat." A Vietnamese woman, formerly a classical dancer in Hanoi, has become the mistress of a French functionary. With her eye on the narrator, while her "proprietor" sleeps nearby, she performs a dance that the narrator interprets as a dance of combat—a dance of resistance to her present state, a dance of remorse or regret for this life among Frenchmen. Conveying the effect of dance resists the written word. The story gives the narrator's interpretation of what he sees. He is ready to liken her dramatic skill to that of Sarah Bernhardt on the stage. This appears to mean nothing to the Vietnamese woman, Muoï, but it coincides with her most subtle acting—not her dance but her attempt afterward to pass it off as just a display of artistry. As an indication that her combat was much more than technique, the story ends with a reminder of her imprisonment: the words "Muoï's proprietor."

Of course, in one form, Vietnamese dance and theater evoked the people's history and their pride, their ancient struggle against Chinese invaders.[90] To have been on the stage in Hanoi, as Muoï had been, was to know political, nationalistic theater, and the narrator links her departure from the stage to a French officer, her earlier "proprietor." She had acquired "somewhere and somehow" a wardrobe of "the finest and gayest of silk garments." The narrator leaves little doubt about where and how. Muoï's first dance may be, as the narrator suggests, combat with the spirit of the bygone officer. In the second part she confronts her own demon spirits, the demons of her feelings about her collaboration with the French. They prevail. She is defeated. She returns to her latest domestic arrangement.[91]

Governor-General de Lanessan wrote in his report of October 30, 1891: "I take the liberty of considering the delta today as pacified."[92] Whatever he might tell Paris about the Red River delta, he could not convince soldiers. O'Neill left Tonkin a few months later, believing that resistance to the French would persist for "a long time." He returned to Algeria for a while, then was discharged from the legion in 1892. He brought away an intermittent "fever," as malaria was often called.[93] The narrator contracts fever in the story "Slovatski," but, unlike the title character, he recovers. During his time in Tonkin and back in Algeria, O'Neill

90. Jules Boissière, *Fumeurs d'opium* (Paris, 1896), 45–151; Louis Peytral, *Silhouettes tonkinoises* (Paris, 1897), 237–56; Isoart, *Le phénomène national vietnamien,* 47–48.

91. Ann Laura Stoler, "Sexual Affronts and Racial Frontiers: European Identities and the Cultural Politics of Exclusion in Colonial Southeast Asia," *Comparative Studies in Society and History* 34 (July 1992): 530.

92. Quoted in Robert Marle, "La pacification du Tonkin (1891–1896)," *Bulletin de la société des études indochinoises de Saigon* 47 (1972): 60.

93. James O'Neill to Fred Holland Day, July 7, 1895, Copeland and Day Papers, American Antiquarian Society.

xlvi | JAMES O'NEILL: FOREIGN LEGIONNAIRE AND WRITER

knew a Hungarian legionnaire, Harry Kopperl. O'Neill went to the United States, and Kopperl went to Budapest. Three years later, in the spring of 1895, Kopperl persuaded O'Neill to return to Europe, with Budapest as his destination. By then, O'Neill had begun to think that he might make a living by writing. In 1894 the British periodical *Good Words* had published his essay "The Great Buddha." O'Neill was about to sail from New York when Fred Holland Day agreed to publish *Garrison Tales from Tonquin.*

O'Neill's sister, Sister Frances of the Society of St. Margaret, had become a leading member of her order. In addition to Children's Hospital in Boston, the sisters managed the Wellesley Convalescent Home. Beginning in 1881 Sister Frances was superintendent of St. Barnabas's Hospital in Newark, New Jersey, for nine years.[94] In Boston, Sister Teresa gave up the position of superintendent of Children's Hospital in 1888. O'Neill knew her, as did Fred Holland Day. O'Neill thought in 1895 that if Sister Teresa learned from Day that O'Neill intended to go to Europe, she would tell Sister Frances, who would try to dissuade him.

O'Neill spent some time at Priory Farm near Verbank in Dutchess County, New York, where he spoke of "clearing up my old tracks," as he prepared to leave for Europe.[95] This was the site of St. Paul's Training School, which provided "industrial training for boys." The school was one of the charities of the Brothers of Nazareth, a lay order in the Episcopal Church, founded in 1886. Its rich patron, General John Watts de Peyster, donated land, then erected a building designed to house forty boys. The brothers devoted themselves to "prayer and manual work." They also took part in "highly ritualistic" Anglo-Catholic services, which they, like the Cowley Fathers, traced to a Catholic tradition in the English Church, not to Rome. St. Paul's Training School for Boys

94. Clement A. Smith, *The Children's Hospital of Boston* (Boston, 1983), 85–96; Sister Catherine Louise, *The House of My Pilgrimage: History of the American House of the Society of St. Margaret: 1873–1973* (Glenside, Pa., [1972]), 21–88; "Hospital St. Barnabas," *St. Margaret's Quarterly* (April 1921): 10–11.

95. James O'Neill to Fred Holland Day, May 2, 1895, Copeland and Day Papers, American Antiquarian Society.

JAMES O'NEILL: FOREIGN LEGIONNAIRE AND WRITER | xlvii

was founded in 1894; however, the Brothers of Nazareth survived as an order for only a few more years.[96]

In 1894 Robert Nisbet Bain, a linguist and an employee of the British Museum, published an English translation of *Eyes Like the Sea*, a novel by the grand old man of Hungarian letters, Mór Jókai, usually known in English as Maurus Jókai. Although Bain took the lead in bringing Jókai's work to English-speaking readers, even he had read only twenty-five of Jókai's 150 novels. Bain admired him for his freedom from the "pessimistic tone of Continental fiction" and from the "mental vivisection" of "Ibsenism."[97] By the time James O'Neill booked passage to Europe in 1895, he had taken an interest in Hungarian literature. He hoped to learn Hungarian and to spend two years in Budapest, writing about contemporary Hungarian authors. His Hungarian friends in New York praised his progress with the language. Maurus Jókai was better known to Americans in the 1890s than he was a hundred years later. His admirers included O'Neill, for whom he represented the prolific, successful, politically engaged author. Did O'Neill imagine his future self? He later wrote of Jókai: "Literature had become his true vocation."[98]

O'Neill sailed for Europe in the first week of June 1895. To avoid cholera in Naples he left the ship in Genoa and went to Lucerne for a few days with someone he had met on board. He

96. James Elliott Lindsley, *This Planted Vine: A Narrative History of the Episcopal Diocese of New York* (New York, 1984), 253; Charles Lewis Slattery, *David Hummell Greer: Eighth Bishop of New York* (New York, 1921), 202–4; Frank Allaben, *John Watts de Peyster* (New York, 1908), 2:219–22; *New York Times,* Feb. 3, 16, 1896; Floyd Appleton, *Church Philanthropy in New York* (New York, 1906), 80; Anson, *Call of the Cloister,* 543–44.

97. Maurus Jókai, *Eyes Like the Sea,* trans. R. Nisbet Bain (New York, 1894), ix-xi.

98. O'Neill, "Maurus Jókai," *The Critic* 31 (Nov. 6, 1897): 261.; John Bell Henneman, "The Nestor of Hungarian Letters," *Sewanee Review* 4 (Feb. 1896): esp. 190–91; "A Literary Journal," *The Bookman* 5 (June 1897): 283–84; Neltje Blanchau, "Dr. Maurice Jókai: A Sketch," *The Critic* 33 (Sept. 1898): 167–70; Francis Magyar, "Jókai's Reception in England and America," *American Slavic and East European Review* 17 (Oct. 1958): 332–45; Lóránt Czigány, "Jókai's Popularity in Victorian England," *New Hungarian Quarterly* 16 (1975): 186–92.

reached Budapest in the first week of July but failed to find Harry Kopperl, who had been transferred by his employer. O'Neill thought of returning to New York, but he suffered a recurrence of malaria in Venice. During this delay he received an offer of employment as a private tutor in Vienna. He hoped to support himself partly by teaching English; Viennese German was familiar to him, he said, because he had learned German from "a Jew from Vienna."[99] He sent Day travel essays about Budapest and Vienna, asking Day to arrange publication. For a while he lived on ten cents a day, and he said he might reenlist in the French Army. But in September, O'Neill went back to Budapest, where he at last found Harry Kopperl and began teaching English in a newly opened Berlitz school.

Garrison Tales from Tonquin was published in November; O'Neill did not receive his copies until the end of February 1896. This delay distressed him because he had promised to send a copy to a former *adjudant* of the Foreign Legion in Paris. Adjutant Hauck, O'Neill said, "had always been heavenly kind to me,"[100] and Hauck's brother-in-law later translated the tales into French so that Hauck could read them. O'Neill took hope from a short-lived proposal to publish the translation, giving him "the honour (!) of appearing in the language of Molière forsooth!" He wrote more stories set in Algeria. By March 1896 he had decided to return to New York in June. He had failed to master Hungarian, and he had heard of "an open[in]g" in New York. Still, he said he would return to Budapest "if I don't succeed in N.Y."[101]

Returning to the United States, O'Neill went by way of Oxford to visit the Cowley Fathers in late June 1896. For a mailing address he gave Day the name of Father George Congreve, second to Father Benson in the society. A church historian contrasts the

99. James O'Neill to Fred Holland Day, July 7, 1895, Copeland and Day Papers, American Antiquarian Society.

100. James O'Neill to Fred Holland Day, Feb. 22, 1896, Fred Holland Day Papers, Norwood Historical Society.

101. James O'Neill to Fred Holland Day, May 24, 1896, ibid.

two priests—Benson "strong and apparently harsh," Congreve "sensitive and seemingly delicate."[102] O'Neill narrowly missed the celebration of the new conventual church of St. John the Evangelist, built of Bath stone in the Gothic style. The fathers told visitors that their ceremony was "founded on the Use of Sarum."[103] A few years later, George Santayana visited Cowley and spent some time at what he called the fathers' "toy monastery." The spectacle of Anglican monks at the start of the twentieth century—trying to recreate the forms of an era of belief in a worldly England—left him unpersuaded. He respected the priests as "souls in need of religion," who were "groping for expression and for support." But he scorned what he saw as "a silly aesthetic sensual side, all vanity and pose and ritualistic pedantry."[104] To Santayana the Cowley Fathers were playacting, not rediscovering medieval faith.

James O'Neill left no record of further dealings with Copeland and Day after the summer of 1896, and the track of his move-

102. A. M. Allchin, *The Silent Rebellion: Anglican Religious Communities, 1845–1900* (London, 1958), 231. See also Michael Hill, *Religious Order: A Study of Virtuoso Religion and Its Legitimation in the Nineteenth-Century Church of England* (London, 1973), 52, 239, 305; M. V. Woodgate, *Father Congreve of Cowley* (London, 1956).

103. Entry of June 15, 1896, Mountstuart E. Grant Duff, *Notes from a Diary: 1896 to January 23, 1901* (New York, 1905), 1:73; Anson, *Call of the Cloister*, 72–73; B. P. Wolffe, "Cowley," in *A History of the County of Oxford*, ed. Mary D. Lobel (Oxford, 1957), 5:93; William Maskell, *The Ancient Liturgy of the Church of England*, 3d ed. (Oxford, 1882), iv–vii, lxxvii–lxxix.

104. George Santayana to Sturgis de Sastre, Aug. 23, 1901, *The Letters of George Santayana*, ed. William G. Holzberger (Cambridge, Mass., 2001), 1:236; George Santayana, *Persons and Places: Fragments of Autobiography*, ed. William G. Holzberger and Herman J. Saatkamp, Jr. (Cambridge, Mass., 1986), 497. Compare T. J. Jackson Lears, *No Place of Grace: Antimodernism and the Transformation of American Culture, 1880–1920* (New York, 1981), 200–9; David Hilliard, "Unenglish and Unmanly: Anglo-Catholicism and Homosexuality," *Victorian Studies* 25 (1982): 181–210; Cuthbert Wright, "Out of Harm's Way: Some Notes on the Esthetic Movement of the Nineties," *The Bookman* 70 (Nov. 1929): 234–43; Mrs. W. Pitt Byrne, *Social Hours with Celebrities* (London, 1898), 1:273n.

ments disappears in the Bronx. In response to his inquiry about sales of *Garrison Tales from Tonquin,* Day sent a check for $7.50, an amount which would have covered author's royalties on sixty copies if sales had reached a level to yield royalties. Of course, the book did not come near repaying the cost of production; Day debited his check as a cash loan. O'Neill's last letters bordered on the churlish, as he evidently realized that he could not support himself as a man of letters and that there would be no volume of *Algerian Tales.*

O'Neill parted from Copeland and Day with some mystery. He gave his address as "the Fordham Press 185th St. and 3d Ave."[105] No record survives of a "Fordham Press" in 1896—no printer, no publisher, no newspaper; and maps of the Bronx show that 185th Street did not intersect with Third Avenue in 1896, but stopped at Washington Avenue. Still, O'Neill somehow received at least one more letter from Day. In 1898 O'Neill's sister spent two months in Puerto Rico, nursing American soldiers in the war with Spain. She published an account of the experience in her society's magazine.[106] She ended her nursing career at St. Mark's Home in Philadelphia. Sister Frances died on October 8, 1917. Her brother's letters to her, if they survive, would be the fullest source of information about James O'Neill.

While in Vienna, O'Neill wrote a "biographical sketch" of Maurus Jókai and sent it to Day, asking him "to try to place it for me."[107] Day later mailed it back to O'Neill in New York, and it or another on the same subject became the lead article in the November 6, 1897, issue of *The Critic.* O'Neill had won favor with Jeannette Gilder, editor of *The Critic* in New York and a literary

105. James O'Neill to Fred Holland Day, July 15, 1896, Fred Holland Day Papers, Norwood Historical Society.

106. [Sister Frances], "Hospital Days at Ponce," *St. Margaret's Magazine* 5 (1899): 437–51; entries of Aug. 30–31, Oct. 28, 1898, Convent Diary, Society of St. Margaret, Boston, Massachusetts.

107. James O'Neill to Fred Holland Day, Aug. 6, 1895, Fred Holland Day Papers, Norwood Historical Society; James O'Neill to Fred Holland Day, July 7, 1895, Copeland and Day Papers, American Antiquarian Society.

agent. An independent woman "of strong personality," she often wore clothes her contemporaries thought "mannish." She was known for her solicitude: "out of her great, kind heart she helped struggling authors." She had published Copeland and Day's announcement of *Garrison Tales from Tonquin* in her issue of November 2, 1895. *The Critic* had a circulation of 5,500—ahead of *The Bookman's* 1,096 but far behind *Harper's* 165,000. Twenty years later, a journalist wrote: "Her magazine, *The Critic*, is forgotten, but in its day it exerted a tremendous influence and had much to do with shaping more than one important literary career."[108] In her caption for a portrait of Jókai, Gilder called O'Neill's work "a vivid sketch."[109] But "Maurus Jókai" appears to have been the close of O'Neill's career as a man of letters.

Did O'Neill recall his own methods as he described Jókai's? "Indeed, during the half-century of his literary career, Jókai has seen strange sights and heard strange things; and it is not to be wondered at if they have got into his books. He never disdained hints; here a word from one, there a tale from another; all was grist that came to his mill, and from the rough uncouth material he produced beautiful results." O'Neill told Day about his time in the Foreign Legion: "my experiences were strange, some of them."[110] A writer transmuted strangeness into literature. Who can doubt that O'Neill sought to produce beautiful results from rough, uncouth material? For him, the words "beauty" and "beautiful" always connote harmony, symmetry, the picturesque. He could have said, with William Dean Howells: "Beauty and truth have been my aim, and simple as these things seem they are the tyrants

108. L. Frank Tooker, *The Joys and Tribulations of an Editor* (New York, 1924), 100; William Webster Ellsworth, *A Golden Age of Authors: A Publisher's Recollection* (Boston, 1919), 141; Sidney Kramer, *A History of Stone & Kimball and Herbert S. Stone & Co.* (Chicago, 1940), 53n.; Isaac F. Marcosson, *Adventures in Interviewing* (New York, 1919), 275; Frank Luther Mott, *A History of American Magazines*, vol. 4, *1885–1905* (Cambridge, Mass., 1957), 124.

109. *The Critic* 31 (Nov. 6, 1897): 268.

110. James O'Neill to Fred Holland Day, June 1, 1895, Copeland and Day Papers, American Antiquarian Society.

of art."[111] O'Neill's narrator sometimes hints at a grimmer, darker experience—truth that he could not make into beauty—as in "De Perier," when he reacts to the notion of reenlistment by saying: "Why, you might better do anything than become brutalized here in the army!" For the most part, O'Neill's fiction follows his own advice in his unpublished "Introductory": "Now, concerning the Foreign Legion of France, what shall I say? Verily there may be dark pages in its history, but such things are best forgotten."[112] He appears not to have forgotten but also not to have described such things, except briefly, allusively, indirectly. The beauty his art attained was not all of his truth.

O'Neill wishes to engage his readers in his characters' crises of emotion, of identity, and of moral choice. This inquiry extends to the subject of characters' violent deaths—part of the stories' symmetry—but not to a full account of the mark of war on the lives of Vietnamese and legionnaires. His narrator offers a defense of soldiers against the prospect of blame: "Turnkeys and soldiers and hangmen must all shrug their shoulders and disclaim responsibility; and if their hearts ache over it, they, in turn, are to be pitied."[113] Recollecting all that legionnaires had done, or meting out responsibility, would take his fiction too near the "passing strange" truth. O'Neill tries to reconcile sympathy and memory by creating beautiful stories of brutal doings.

Describing one of his unpublished tales, O'Neill wrote: "No moral that I am aware of is evident in it, but it may be *suggestive*

111. *New York Times,* July 26, 1908, reprinted in Ulrich Halfmann, ed., "Interviews with William Dean Howells," *American Literary Realism, 1870–1910* 6 (1973): 363. See also William Dean Howells, *Prefaces to Contemporaries,* ed. George Arms et al. (Gainesville, Fla., 1957); Walter Crane, "Modern Aspects of Life and the Sense of Beauty," in *William Morris to Whistler* (London, 1911), 214; Walter Pater, *Appreciations* [1889], in *Walter Pater: Three Major Texts,* ed. William E. Buckler (New York, 1986), 541–42.

112. "Introductory," in James O'Neill to Fred Holland Day, June 9, 1895, Copeland and Day Papers, American Antiquarian Society.

113. "The Cooly."

of things."[114] This is his favorite method. Nowhere does his story "The Pagoda" announce itself as an attack on imperialism; yet its pages are pervaded by reminders of the evanescence of empires and by mock-serious narrative, which evokes the ludicrousness of the French undertaking in Asia. The critic Alan Sandison later saw a similar cast of mind in the fiction of Kipling: "The British work in India was a huge, macabre joke which Kipling and a few—but only a few—of his characters saw. In the light of this, one's primary duty was only superficially to the Queen-Empress: fundamentally, it was to one's own moral integrity."[115] O'Neill writes of compromised Vietnamese and doomed legionnaires. Some retain or regain their integrity; others do not. He finds beauty in their stories, even in the death of a prisoner of circumstance. But he finds no excuse for France's presence in Indochina. On this subject his way to be "suggestive" is to hold the imperial venture up to ridicule.

O'Neill admired the paintings of Walter Crane. When a traveling exhibit came to Vienna, O'Neill saw it in the Imperial Austrian Museum of Art and Industry on July 7, 1895. He wrote to Day: "I gloated on it."[116] Hailed as a great artist in his own time, Crane believed that art must exert influence toward a socialist future, harmonious and egalitarian. He wrote: "The arts, like humanity, do not flourish under Imperial rule." Praising colleagues who depicted "aspects of labour under modern conditions," he nevertheless turned his efforts in another direction.[117] His works, George

114. James O'Neill to Fred Holland Day, Sept. 10, 1895, Fred Holland Day Papers, Norwood Historical Society.

115. Alan Sandison, "Kipling: The Artist and the Empire," in *Kipling's Mind and Art: Selected Critical Essays,* ed. Andrew Rutherford (Stanford, Calif., 1964), 161. See also Alan Sandison, *The Wheel of Empire: A Study of the Imperial Idea in Some Late Nineteenth and Early Twentieth-Century Fiction* (New York, 1967), esp. chap. 4.

116. James O'Neill to Fred Holland Day, July 7, 1895, Copeland and Day Papers, American Antiquarian Society.

117. Walter Crane, "The Socialist Ideal as a New Inspiration in Art," in *William Morris to Whistler,* 88, 92.

Bernard Shaw wrote in 1895, "treat scenes of life and character in a decorative way," one with an underlying orderly design.[118] Crane's ideal symmetry drew upon symbol, allegory, and myth, rather than naturalistic portrayal of "social degradation." His ambitions for modern society found expression in his "search for a new harmony, a higher sense of beauty." Maurus Jókai praised Crane for striving "to ennoble popular art."[119] Like Crane, O'Neill strove for betterment through optimism. Crane sought the ideal in the human; O'Neill saw flaws and failures, which he portrayed with the ideal in view.

Before its publication, O'Neill imagined that his book of tales might "succeed."[120] By this he meant a commercial success, justifying publication of a second book of fiction by James O'Neill. His mind's eye saw readers who understood his tales: the fight in Tonkin would continue as long as the Vietnamese exist or "until justice and equity reign in the East." He wished to attract "the notice of our Occidental minds" to this attribute of the people he had fought. Americans and Europeans ought to know that the Vietnamese, instead of being "savages," were "patriots"; they had "made desperate efforts to resist French invasion," and this "resistance to injustice" both "preserved individuality" and proved "a certain superiority."[121] Such an idea could not gain "notice" if the book did not "succeed." To this end, O'Neill wrote stories of individuals. Among reviewers, only the *Hartford Courant*'s critic perceived that the book's "vivid, pathetic pictures" were all con-

118. George Bernard Shaw, *The Sanity of Art* (London, 1908), 26.

119. Walter Crane, *An Artist's Reminiscences* (New York, 1907), 336, 471; Isobel Spencer, *Walter Crane* (New York, 1975); Peter Stansky, *Redesigning the World: William Morris, the 1880s, and the Arts and Crafts* (Princeton, N.J., 1985), 196–97; Greg Smith, "Developing a Public Language of Art," in *Walter Crane 1845–1915: Artist, Designer, and Socialist*, ed. Greg Smith and Sarah Hyde (London, 1989), 13–23.

120. James O'Neill to Fred Holland Day, June 1, 1895, Copeland and Day Papers, American Antiquarian Society.

121. "Introductory," in James O'Neill to Fred Holland Day, June 9, 1895, Copeland and Day Papers, American Antiquarian Society.

nected to one theme: the French "yoke." The critic said of O'Neill: "The writer knows his theme."[122] It emerges most overtly in "Père Loraine," most subtly in "The Pagoda." But *Garrison Tales from Tonquin* was not destined to succeed in the 1890s, either in sales or in broadening the perspective of "Occidental minds."

As the United Sates made itself an imperial power in Asia after its war with Spain in 1898, some Americans recalled France's experience with empire. An admirer of France and of the Foreign Legion, George Woodberry of Columbia University wrote: "In the course of years she found herself saddled with a burden of colonial empire as awkwardly and reluctantly as was the case with us and the Philippines. . . . The vitalizing and beneficent power of French civilization, as it might almost seem against the will of its masters, dominates a vast track of doubtful empire. . . . The policy of pacification and penetration is, indeed, one of the present glories of France."[123] On the other hand, Henry E. Bourne of Western Reserve University shared O'Neill's outlook. In the spring of 1899 he published an essay "to show how instructive this French enterprise should prove to us," while Americans asserted control over the Philippine Islands. He wrote of France's mistakes and frustrated expectations in Indochina: "The bad quarter of an hour comes when peoples annexed or purchased cease to be numbers, and become men, when they reject the alien civilization thrust upon them, and when punitive expeditions and mobile columns and every variety of petty warfare crowd into the expense account, leaving the empire-builders each year some millions in debt." An attempt at conquest and "civilizing" grew difficult and expensive, as O'Neill, too, had mentioned; it also contradicted the devotion to liberty proclaimed by France and the United States. Bourne wrote: "The attempt to force a people into the mould of a foreign civilization is a subtle and deadly attack upon native rights—unless, indeed, rights are the sole property of men of Eu-

122. *Hartford Courant,* Dec. 19, 1895.
123. George E. Woodberry, *North Africa and the Desert: Scenes and Moods* (New York, 1914), 41–42.

ropean race."[124] In other words, liberty could not light the world by conquest, even if conquerors professed to pursue enlightened policies.

France, according to some critics of American empire, already showed the effects of ill-advised imperial adventures. More explicit and polemical than O'Neill in his tales, anti-imperial writers dwelt on the drain of France's wealth into colonies. Undertaking a vain scheme of aggrandizement, the French sent time-servers and crass opportunists to operate the empire. The journalist Herbert Adams Gibbons wrote that French colonial functionaries "seem to be bearing the white man's burden for the salary they get out of it."[125] Other censure warned that France was succumbing to militarism, a consequence of building an army to hold an empire.[126] Empires and armies, critics warned, sapped national character and racial vitality.[127] Toward all these misfortunes the United States would move if the country followed the example of European imperial expansion.

Thornton Van Vliet distilled this threatened transformation of America into his question: What should be done with the Statue of Liberty? Should it be dismantled and returned to France? Should it be recast into smaller copies to be erected "in our conquered islands to impress the natives with the benevolence of our institutions?" Should it be given a sword rather than a torch and be renamed "Liberty Conquering the World?" Van Vliet concluded

124. Henry E. Bourne, "A French Colonial Experiment in the Far East," *Yale Review* 8 (May 1899): 8, 27. See also Henry E. Bourne, "Lessons from the Recent History of European Dependencies," *Annual Report of the American Historical Association for the Year 1898* (Washington, D.C., 1899), 303–12.

125. Herbert Adams Gibbons, *The New Map of Asia* (New York, 1919), 110.

126. William Graham Sumner, "The Conquest of the United States by Spain," in *On Liberty, Society, and Politics,* ed. Robert C. Bannister (Indianapolis, Ind., 1992), 289.

127. Frank Ninkovich, *The United States and Imperialism* (Oxford, 2001), 45; David Starr Jordan, *Imperial Democracy* (New York, 1899), 94; Charles Dudley Warner, *A Roundabout Journey* (Boston, 1884), 5–6; John Griffin Carlisle, "Our Future Policy," *Harper's New Monthly Magazine* 97 (Oct. 1898): 724–26.

that the statue had become "very inappropriate to the present situation and . . . a very awkward object to have in sight."[128] As Filipinos fought American occupation, American officers advocated more aggressive, harsher measures to impose pacification. General Samuel Young called these practices "European methods," described by the French in publications he had studied.[129] Of course, one lesson of experience reiterated in O'Neill's book of tales was the folly of "European methods," which he had seen and used as a private soldier.

George Santayana dismissed objections such as Van Vliet's. Santayana's colleague William James lamented President William McKinley's decisions in favor of empire. James saw them as departures from American principles of self-government expressed in the Declaration of Independence. The United States, James said, had changed its ideals from liberty to empire "in the twinkling of an eye."[130] On the contrary, Santayana later wrote, American history was partly a record of successive aggrandizements, and the United States was preparing in the 1890s for domination beyond its borders, with or without a war against Spain. Santayana did not approve, but he thought that this was "the way of the world since the beginning of time." He called the Declaration of Independence "a piece of literature, a salad of illusions." It might "inspire

128. Quoted in E. Berkeley Tompkins, *Anti-Imperialism in the United States: The Great Debate, 1890–1920* (Philadelphia, 1970), 199.

129. Quoted in Stuart Creighton Miller, *"Benevolent Assimilation": The American Conquest of the Philippines, 1899–1903* (New Haven, Conn., 1982), 162.

130. William James to François Pillon, June 15, 1898, *The Correspondence of William James,* ed. Ignas K. Skrupskelis and Elizabeth M. Berkeley (Charlottesville, Va., 1992–), 8:372. See also William Dean Howells to Charles Eliot Norton, Aug. 15, 1903, *W. D. Howells: Selected Letters,* vol. 5, *1902–1911,* ed. William C. Fischer and Christoph K. Lohmann (Boston, 1983), 61; William Roscoe Thayer to Walter Hines Page, May 31, 1904, *The Letters of William Roscoe Thayer,* ed. Charles Downer Hazen (Boston, 1926), 102–3; Harry Thurston Peck, "About the War," *The Bookman* 7 (June 1898): 321–27, esp. 325–26; Lawrence J. Oliver, *Brander Matthews, Theodore Roosevelt, and the Politics of American Literature, 1880–1920* (Knoxville, Tenn., 1992), 68–69.

a Rousseau but it cannot guide a government." In believing that it had guided America's government until 1898, William James "held a false moralistic view of history," Santayana concluded; James did not understand his own country's past.[131]

The America James O'Neill wished to reach with his stories of empire's effects had not remained simply a virtuous, unselfish republic for 125 years. Nor did the United States need to undergo some process of becoming like France before it would assert its power overseas with force. Most Americans expressed no objections to their government's actions in Asia. Opposition to war against Filipinos and censure of American empire, though eloquent, attracted little support in the United States. Public attention to Asia ran mainly along channels of exoticism not far from those that had attracted Fred Holland Day. O'Neill's cautionary tales reached neither William James and his allies nor sentimental American readers engaged by romantic adventures set in "Oriental" lands, in the manner of the fiction of Pierre Loti.

Fred Holland Day admired the work of Julien Viaud, the French naval officer who published under the pen name Pierre Loti. Day praised his "sympathy . . . for those souls cast out by humanity" and bestowed the highest compliment by invoking Keats in a summary of Loti's achievement. The novel of Japan, *Madame Chrysanthème,* and other works demonstrated, Day wrote, Loti's perception of an "imperishable rhythm in the hearts of those who appreciate that Truth which is Beauty."[132] As O'Neill's book sank into oblivion, *Madame Chrysanthème*—which Thomas Sergeant Perry, writing from Tokyo, called "simply loathsome"—was yielding material for an American short story by John Luther Long,

131. Santayana, *Persons and Places,* ed. Holzberger and Saatkamp, 402–4; Hans-Joachim Lang, "Course of Empire: Four Harvard Perspectives on Imperialism," in *An American Empire: Expansionist Cultures and Policies, 1881–1917,* ed. Serge Ricard (Aix-en-Provence, 1990), 167–85.

132. [Fred Holland Day], "Concerning Recent Books and Bookmaking," *The Knight Errant* 1 (Oct. 1892): 93–94, reprinted in *F. Holland Day: Selected Texts and Bibliography,* ed. Verna Posever Curtis and Jane Van Nimmen (New York, 1995), 34–35.

"Madame Butterfly."[133] In 1900 David Belasco adapted Long's story into a successful play; four years later, as Giacomo Puccini's opera, *Madama Butterfly,* it started its world travels.[134] After attending the first American production of the opera, Long reported with satisfaction that the audience "had seven fits about it."[135] Thus began a national tour of *Madama Butterfly,* with more than two hundred performances in six months.[136]

133. Pierre Loti [Julien Viaud], *Madame Chrysanthème* (Paris, 1888); Virginia Harlow, *Thomas Sergeant Perry: A Biography* (Durham, N.C., 1950), 172; John Luther Long, "Madame Butterfly," *Century Magazine* 55 (Jan. 1898): 374–92; Jan van Rij, *Madame Butterfly: Japonisme, Puccini, and the Search for the Real Cho-Cho-San* (Berkeley, Calif., 2001).

134. For performances see Alfred Loewenberg, comp., *Annals of Opera, 1597–1940* (Cambridge, 1943), 656.

135. John [Luther Long] to [Albert Bigelow Paine], [Oct. 1906], AP 1021, Albert Bigelow Paine Papers, Henry E. Huntington Library, San Marino, California.

136. Vincent Seligman, *Puccini among Friends* (New York, 1938), 96, 100.

EDITOR'S NOTE

I have retained the spellings of the original edition, including James O'Neill's phonetic renderings of Vietnamese words. The following corrections have been made:

Roebke

PAGE 5   "Ich hatt' einen Kameraden." [*"Ich hatt einen Kam-eraden."* (1895)] From "Der gute Kamerad" in Ludwig Uhland, *Werke,* ed. Hans-Rüdiger Schwab (Frankfurt am Main, 1983), 1:160.

PAGE 5   mustn't [musn't (1895)]

PAGE 10   infirmarians [informarians (1895)]

Homesickness

PAGE 21   Arab's [Arabs' (1895)]

PAGE 23   George Dandin [Georges Daudin (1895)]

PAGE 27   ['words are indeed the physicians of a distempered feeling' (1895)]
          O'Neill's chosen version of Aeschylus, *Prometheus Bound,* lines 379–80.

Slovatski

PAGE 29   *Légionnaires [Legionnaires* (1895)]

PAGE 33   *Légionnaires [Legionnaires* (1895)]

A Spiritual Combat

PAGE 37   in a soft, purring, twittering way, suggestive of birds, yet without being strictly musical [of birds, yet without being strictly musical in a soft, purring, twittering way, suggestive (1895)]

Eckermann and Tannemeyer

PAGE 54   Lanessan [Lanassan (1895)]

A Dream

De Perier

The Worst of the Bargain

The Pagoda

Maurus Jókai

Garrison Tales from Tonquin

To Sister Frances
Erewhile Mary O'Neill
With her brother's dearest love

INTRODUCTORY

With China and Japan the world has at length grown familiar; in as far as the Occident can comprehend the Orient, the daily life of the Mongolian race has been made known to us.

There are, however, some branches of this race of which little is said. Since 1884 the French have had possession of the northern province of Annam, and it is this part of the extreme Orient that the following short tales may serve to illustrate. Even in this province of Tonkin,—or Tonquin, as we write it in English,—the Annamites are divided into several distinct peoples; but how each may differ from the other would be a problem for the ethnographer. French rule was not gratefully accepted in Tonquin. These poor "savages" did not at once comprehend or appreciate the honor of being subject to France; so they made desperate efforts to resist French invasion.

France professed to have right as well as might, and said, forsooth, that it was to free the poor Annamites from Chinese cruelty and injustice that she stepped in. The Annamites having grown used to Chinese authority, doubtless considered that the devil they knew would be better than the one they did not know, and that to exchange Chinese government for French would be to fall from the frying-pan into the fire; and accordingly they made what resistance was possible.

Those who survived the struggle accepted their new masters with the resignation of the rat that welcomed death when the trap snapped.

But not all of them: since many banded themselves together, and fled to the mountains, where they built strongholds in which defiance is still offered to French invaders. Similar "piratical" bands had always made similar resistance to Chinese rule, and until justice and equity reign in the East, or until the Annamite race dies out, piracy or brigandage will probably flourish in Tonquin.

Already France has made great changes in this country; she has spent millions of money, expecting an adequate profit, but the profit has not yet appeared; and more than once she may have repented of her generosity (!) and wished to retreat; but that such men as Admiral Courbet, Francis Garnier, and others, should have lost their lives for naught would be too lamentable; and having involved herself so far, retreat would be too great a disaster.

By the force of her army, France maintains her hold on Tonquin.

In Parisian newspapers you may read that Tonquin is pacified, and a quibbling explanation will be made when the news arrives that such and such an officer has been killed by the "pirates." No; Tonquin is not yet pacified, and it will probably be a long time before these bands of pirates or patriots cease to exist.

The Annamite religion is Buddhism; the language is as different from Chinese as French is from Italian; it is a monosyllabic language, and in some ways very simple and easy to learn, while in others, it is exceedingly difficult. The differences between Annamite and Chinese dress, customs, arts and sciences, etc., are marked; but that the Annamites have been materially influenced by the Chinese is evident. Inferior to the Chinese they certainly are, but this is probably the result of long subjection, rather than of innate mediocrity. That the Annamite is not an abject or cowardly race is evident from the fact that resistance to injustice continues to be made; and that it has preserved individuality in so many instances seems proof of a certain superiority; and so it seems to me that it merits the notice of our Occidental minds.

ROEBKE

"Ich hatt' einen Kameraden."

One day I sat cleaning my rifle,—trying to clean it rather, and not succeeding at all. We had been out at target practise, and now with dry rags I was trying to remove the soot from the barrel.

From my soul I loathed the work, and my disgust must have been apparent in my face, for Roebke came forward and took it from me.

"O, but you mustn't wet the rags," I exclaimed, for I saw him dip the one on the end of the ramrod into a basin of water.

"Why not, pray?" he asked.

"Because some moisture might be left on the inside of the barrel, and that would cause rust."

"*Might* be left, yes; but I do not intend to leave any. The time you spend in trying to get the soot out in your way will not be needed in getting all the moisture out in my way."

Very dexterously he did the job, and in a little while my rifle was shining; fit to pass the inspection of a gunsmith.

"You see," he went on, "if one will be careful and exact, he may use expedients which are forbidden to others; one need not always choose the hardest method of doing a thing because it is the safest; of course a bad swimmer must walk around and cross on the bridge, but if you can swim as well as you can walk, why, you may plunge in and get across first. You may even have your clothes dry before the other fellow arrives."

Roebke was not given to talking much, and this little spurt of philosophy surprised me. He had been at Gex for a month, but I had never noticed him particularly. He and Dare had arrived with a detachment of *"bleus,"* and they had been put into our squad.

Now, Dare was a handsome, loud-spoken fellow, so all our attention was given to him; and in this way Roebke had come among us unnoticed.

"Come on!" I said, "if water is good for rifles, then wine is good for us. Come on, I'll pay you a *quart.*"

This was a weak joke; still I was surprised at the way he took it.

"O, excuse me," he said, "I did not clean your rifle in order to earn a drink."

"I did not suppose so, either," I retorted, "or I would not have let you do it. Now don't stop me from liking you. Besides, you may pay for the *quart* yourself if you are so very stiff-necked." Then he excused his speech and we went off to the canteen.

If I had thought to draw him out over one glass of wine it was because I did not know my man.

As we talked together,—I believe we talked shop mostly on that occasion, but some people can talk of logarithms and make them interesting,—as we talked, I say, I wondered at my lack of perception. How was it that I had given my attention to the addle-headed Dare, and overlooked Roebke? Well, henceforth I would repair my error; and, indeed, Dare quite faded from my horizon, and Roebke grew great before me. Desmond, who was an unobserving Irishman, once asked me why I wasted my time talking to Roebke, and I said: "O, there is no accounting for taste, you know; some waste their time one way and some another. Every one cannot be interested in Gaboriau's novels." And so, every evening, all that Algerian summer, Roebke and I would sit on Esther's tomb in the old Jewish cemetery of Gex, and talk of everything human and divine.

Before the summer was gone we had grown somewhat familiar with each other, so once I ventured to ask: "What brought you into the French army, Roebke?"

He looked at me in a strange way, and said slowly: "Do you wish me to tell you?"

After a moment's consideration I replied: "No, perhaps you had better not; on second thoughts I am sure you had better not. Please forget that I asked you about it." But he did not forget, and our companionship was somewhat spoiled after that: he was wishful to tell me the story of his life, and I was anxious to prevent him. After that I was employed in the *Bureau des entrées* at the hospital, and I saw little more of Roebke for a time. Then, with mystery in his manner, he came to me one evening and asked me to come and talk with him.

The summer had passed and the night air was cold, but we went again and sat on Esther's tomb. Thistles gone to seed and dry grasses made the place look desolate; we might have gone to the canteen, or to a Moorish coffee-house, but unconsciously we went to the old spot.

"You know," Roebke began, "that I am going to Tonquin."

"No, I did not know," said I; "but I think you are wise. I am thinking of asking to go myself."

"O, will you? I wish you would," he cried. "If you come I need not tell you yet."

"Need not tell me what?" I asked.

"Why, the story of my life; how I came to be here."

"But, my dear fellow, you need not tell me in any case, need you? True, I was curious for half a minute,—you seem to be so well fitted for a better life; but now, believe me, I have not the least wish to know; and consider this," I went on, "in your life you may have committed some crime; you may have worked some evil; if it were so and if I knew it I might say—I would say, knowing your present character as I do—that nothing in your past could ever make any difference in my regard for you now. Yes, I would say this, and I would mean it too; yet, try as I might, I should not be able to forget what you might tell me; it would influence my thoughts of you in spite of myself, and I would regard you accordingly. No doubt this seems selfish in me, to object to hearing your story; but I know myself a little, and I know you a little. Evil, yes, there is plenty of evil in all of our lives, and my belief is that the wisest course is to hide it,—to put it away as far as we can,—out of sight. It will spread if we tell of it. Of course confession would give relief: sins always seem smaller when we talk them over. I have concluded that the right punishment for our evil deeds is to be obliged to keep them hidden."

All this time Roebke listened in silence; already it was too dark for me to see the expression of his face. At last he said: "How romantic you are! I did not say there was any crime or any evil in my past life, did I?"

"O, no; nor did I say there had been. I only said that if it were so I did not wish to know it."

"Well, there has been evil," he said, "but not of my doing. If what I have to tell you regarded only myself, I should not hesitate for an instant; but others are involved, and so I hesitate. Now, if you are coming to Tonquin, I will postpone my story. I can tell you on the ship, or after we arrive. If I had known you intended to come I would not have called you out to-night. You see I have decided to go, and I shall probably never return. I wanted some one to hear my story; some one who would understand and know how to act; some one I can trust."

"But hold on, Roebke," I exclaimed, "you think I am such a one? Indeed, you mistake." He interrupted my protest and began to talk Schopenhauer. Finally he came back.

"One thing I will tell you now," he said. "I wear a wallet attached by a cord about my neck,—after the manner of German soldiers who carry their money in that way. Now, there is no money in my wallet, but there is a ring, and some writing; it is a writing in cipher, with a key which you can easily understand. If you hear of my death, please try to obtain possession of this wallet, and act, if you can, as the writing will instruct."

"Well, Roebke," I said, "a minute ago you accused me of being romantic, but with your ring and your cryptogram you seem doubly so. But why do you talk of death? Thousands who go to Tonquin never come back, I admit; but that is no reason why you and I should not come back, if we go. However, if it will relieve your mind, I promise to do as you wish."

The moon had arisen, and lighted up the white tombs around us. The night wind rustled through the dry thistles. A strange, weird feeling was in the air.

I was glad when Roebke stood up. "Let's go and drink to our safe return," he said; so we went off to the canteen. . . .

On the ship there was no chance for Roebke to tell me his story: we were not quartered near each other, and on deck there was always some one else present. "When we arrive," he said. But when we arrived in Tonquin there was still no opportunity; and then we were sent to different posts: he to Yen-Bay and I to Yen-Luong.

Twice I was at Yen-Bay, but I found him absent. On my

third visit I met him, and we talked a little. He was unwell and gloomy.

I tried to arouse him, to bring him out of his phlegmatic indifference, to show him how unhealthy it was to sit moping in such a climate; but he listened to me as if I were far away and he had not understood. Another time I found him when I was on my way to Ka-Dinh, and we, with Fensch and another, spent a few hours together; and then on my return I saw him and made an extra effort to stir him up.

"See here, Roebke," I said, "you will not learn the Annamite language; nay, I do not blame you; but there is no reason why you should not learn English."

When I said that he jumped up and said: "Why, I know English already. Do you know it too?" Sure enough he did. Our surprise was mutual. "Why, oh, why did we not find this out sooner?" he cried, "then I could have told you my story on shipboard and no one else would have been the wiser."

"But it is not too late now, is it?" I asked.

"We have not time for it to-day," he said, "but when will you be up again?"

"I don't know, but surely in a week or so; and I can bring you some English books. You read English?"

"O yes, why—I am an Englishman."

"What! You an Englishman!" I did not believe my ears.

"Yes," he said positively; "but you will understand when you hear my story. Bring me your English books by all means."

It was two weeks before I was sent to Yen-Bay again.

I had some good books,—some of Stevenson's, I think,—and I was anxious for Roebke to have them.

At last an escort was commanded to take something up to Yen-Bay,—money, I believe it was,—some bags of piasters, and I was told to get ready.

Then DeLanny came running to me and begged me to let him go in my stead. He wanted to see his comrade. But I refused; I wanted to see Roebke. Again he pleaded, but I was deaf. What, after waiting so long for a chance? No, DeLanny could wait for his turn as I had done.

On the way I began to ponder and question. What strange thing would Roebke have to tell me? Was it really something worth making so much of a mystery? "Every one," I thought, "imagines his own little experience is of the greatest importance in the world."—"Pshaw," returned my better sense. "Not Roebke; he is a man of genuine commonsense; he does not make mountains of mole-hills; surely it will be an elephant at least that his mountain will give birth to. What sort of elephant, I wonder!"

I learned, on reaching Yen-Bay, that Roebke had gone out with a hunting party, on the route to Ka-Dinh, and that he would return in a few hours. I was tired, so I lay down and went to sleep.

I was awakened by some one who said, "It's Roebke! I tell you it's Roebke!"

"Where? what?" I cried, and I sprang up. Yes, it was Roebke, shot through the breast by a pirate's bullet, and they were bringing him in on a bier. So his premonition was true.

For a time I was stunned; then I said I would help prepare his body for burial. And I remembered his desire: that I should take the wallet with the ring and the writing and do for him as these might explain to me. Already two infirmarians were undressing him, and I ran to them. Yes, there was the wallet on the cord about his neck, as he had said. "I am his friend," I stammered; "he said I could take this wallet; it contains a ring and some writing; that is all; I will show you."

"All right," said one. And then I went to take the wallet, but I staggered back, aghast. I found that the thing about his neck was only the semblance of a wallet, tattooed and painted on the white skin.

I never learned Roebke's story. He is buried on a hill, back of Yen-Bay; his coffin was of woven bamboos, and we put palm branches on his grave.

PÈRE LORAINE

About twenty or thirty years ago there was a new voice heard in Paris. It was not a mighty voice like that of Père Lacordaire, perhaps, but it was like an echo of his voice, full of sweetness and consolation; and no one could hear it unmoved. It spoke to the heart rather than to the mind; and so all good women—aye, and all bad women—flocked to hear it. Duchesses and laundresses, Maries and Magdalens, sat down together and listened,—listened till the fire of love was kindled in their hearts; till tenderness and sympathy succeeded pride and scorn; listened till they turned and kissed each other.

It was at Saint Sulpice that Père Loraine began to preach. He was but a young man newly ordained, and no one had ever suspected his power; and no one was more surprised by it than himself.

His life as a student had not been remarkable at all; his superiors and professors had found him somewhat dull in matters of theology, and except that he was clever in geometry and languages, nothing had ever been said of him.

The superior of the Sulpicians had been appointed to preach the Lenten sermons that year, but he fell sick, and his task was given to the young priests in turn, till it was the turn of Père Loraine, and then he preached from mid-Lent till Easter, and Paris listened.

Would he hear confessions? asked the duchesses. Would he advise them in things spiritual? Would he direct them personally? Would he—would he lose his own soul? he asked. No. After Easter he disappeared. Then the duchesses went to the bishop to get him back—and the laundresses would have signed the petition if they had known how to write. Well, the bishop said yes, and Père Loraine came back and preached eight more sermons; and after that Paris heard him no more.

I think he worded his sermons in a very simple manner; and they were mostly about simple everyday matters; only, by his voice and gesture, and by the fire of love and faith which burned in his heart, his words were sublime—on his tongue was the true eloquence.

Of course his bishop sided with the duchesses, and he would have had him remain so as to reflect glory on the church, only Père Loraine decided otherwise. In his youth he had determined to become a missionary, and for this purpose he had learned languages.

To remain in Paris and be adored by fine ladies, yes, that would be delightful; and he could almost convince himself that it was his duty; else why had God given him this power of touching hearts? Such eloquence as converted the people of Paris would be wasted on the barbarians of the Orient. Yes, it really seemed as if God had intended him for this life of ease and elegance in Paris.

But would it last? Could he retain his power over men when his ears and his heart would have become filled with himself? His power, he knew, consisted now in the truth of his purpose,—because he himself felt he could make others feel. But how would it be when flattery had accomplished its work,—when he should no longer see or hear or feel anything but his own magnificence, his own glory? Why, then God's glory would be forgotten, and he would have nothing but empty husks wherewith to feed the people; these they would refuse, and they would turn and rend him. No, a thousand times no: he would leave the duchesses to their own devices, and he would go to Tonquin as a missionary.

Gravely doubting, the bishop assented. I do not know what took his place with the duchesses after that; but, doubtless, they did not lack amusement. As for the laundresses, why, they had their work as usual, I suppose, and that is a great deal. The contention Père Loraine had with his bishop was trifling compared with the struggle he had with himself. Death could claim no greater sacrifice of him than this which he was about to make. It was a death in life which he had chosen. How could he exile himself from all the things he knew and loved?

His mother—yes, and his friend!

O, it was bitter—bitter! . . .

But Christ had called him, and how could he shut his ears to that? How could he make as if he had not heard?

Ah, he *had* heard, and he would obey,—yes, cheerfully. At least his lips should smile, and none should know how his heart might bleed.

Peace would come in time, too; and he would forget his friend and his mother? Why not? Surely God would not forget her, so why need he fret?

But, now, again: should he remain in Paris he might soon become a bishop—the ladies would see to that. And as a bishop, what great powers he would have of serving God and the Church; there would be money to build churches, to educate young men for missionaries. O, money and influence for endless good, whereas now—Back, Satan! Get thee behind me! . . .

Twenty years ago the Far East was not so much in people's minds as it is to-day. Stories of murdered missionaries were heard occasionally, but it was still the West which attracted attention. So Père Loraine was soon forgotten. Sometimes his mother may have heard from him, or sometimes his friend; but very soon communication ceased, and he was as one dead to his sometime friends; yet here he was in Tonquin all this time, about his Father's business. He had been very cautious in his work; first he had assumed the habits and dress of the people; he had learned to wear sandals and a turban. The *Kay-oh* was quite like a cassock anyway, except that it was open at the sides. Then he had learned to eat rice with chopsticks, and sit on the floor while doing it; he could even smoke the Annamite pipe. In this manner he was able to establish a little school in which he began his work of introducing Christianity.

Slow, very slow work it was, and he could never flatter himself with a great result. True, the natives loved him, or they seemed to, and they would say the prayers and make the signs he taught them.

But Buddhism was not supplanted for all of this. Père Loraine felt it and grieved. Did the fault of this lie with him? Not at all; it was in the eternal nature of things that it should be so. The tree which has grown awry for many years may indeed be bent straight, and will remain so while your hand holds it; take your hand away and it will fly back to its natural form. Ah, you say, but its *natural* form is perpendicular! Is it? Who planted it, then? And is *your* straightness perfectly straight? Think! With fire and sword the Spaniards labored for three hundred years to put down idolatry in Mexico, planting Christianity in its stead; yet when an idol was unearthed there a few years ago, it was seen that some one had come in the night and crowned it with flowers. Surely at this rate the worship of Buddha might well withstand twenty years of one man's influence. Aye, for twenty years Père Loraine had labored; and now, with strength and vigor gone, gone so quickly in this strange climate, he still toiled. Ah! if by any means he might save some; for though prematurely old and feeble, his faith and love were still young and strong within him.

During these long years of waiting—of waiting for the end—he had amused himself with one of his old studies; it was a little link to bind him to his past, and to remind him that after all he was a Frenchman and not an Annamite. As a student he had been fond of geometry, and had stood high in the class, and now he made use of his knowledge; here he could put it in practise. Many days and nights he had spent in making maps of his district. Carefully he had traversed the winding paths, through rice-fields and over mountains, from village to village, tracing everything in accurate precision. The natives did not understand it; there were still many things about him which they found strange and unaccountable. This may have caused them to venerate him all the more, or it may have made them mistrust him.

They could remember a time when his speech had been hesitating and uncertain, and even now his accent was peculiar. No, he was not one of themselves, and they did not understand him. No, nor he them: to this day he would ask foolish questions—why they did this or said that—things every one should know without asking. He had told them many strange things, too, such things as were quite true, and yet of themselves they would never have found them out. How had he learned them? Who was he, anyway, this strange man?

Then came the year 1884, and they forgot him. There was something of greater interest to think of. Here was their country being invaded by foreigners. What did it mean? And Père Loraine may have asked the same question: What did it mean? For so many years he had heard no news of Europe; no sign from any western land had appeared; and now it was evident, from the rumors he heard, that some European power was invading Tonquin. Ah, it would be the English, he supposed, spreading farther their conquests in India. But no; it was—yes, it was the French; his own countrymen! What a resurrection of old thoughts for him! What emotions must have filled his breast when he recalled his old, half-forgotten mother-tongue! Ah, how his heart leaped at the thought of speaking it—and being understood. But hold! what would this invasion of Frenchmen mean for this people of his adoption? Would they see a new civilization with favor? Alas, no; for already there was news of much fighting and bloodshed.

He had tried to teach Christian charity to his flock; but he feared they would not be able to submit cheerfully to oppression and to love their enemies. Alas, this is such a hard doctrine to understand, and far harder to practise.

Well, I suppose Père Loraine was very tired of his task, and that his chief desire was to lay it down; and to this end the approach of European civilization must have comforted him, since thereby the march of Christianity would be more rapid. Yet after all was this a positive good? Would his people thrive under a European civilization? He could not tell. Twenty years of Oriental life had changed his new world ideas; thus, to instance a small thing, it seemed now as right and natural to eat his food with chopsticks, as at first it had seemed awkward; of course he would gladly resume the use of knives and forks, but of what benefit would knives and forks be to these Annamites? What benefit had he derived from chopsticks? And by one thing, judge of all the rest.

When will we learn that the manners and customs which differ from our own are not, therefore, evil and barbarous? The chief difficulty encountered by the French in their invasion of Tonquin was not the resistance made by the natives; that was indeed a serious check in certain places, so that the lives of many good men were lost by it, but worse than this was the climate of the country, so fatal to Europeans; and then there was the difficulty of the language, so that a right understanding between the French and the Annamites was seldom attained. Next was the difficulty (for the French) of not knowing the roads—not knowing how to get from one place to another. They had maps, it is true, but usually these were inaccurate; thus a mass of irreparable errors was made in every campaign. Very seldom did it happen that a scheme for a combined attack succeeded: companies which should have been in a certain place at a certain time were miles away, wandering vaguely through marshy rice-fields; all because they were mis-guided by the natives, or by their own maps.

It became known to the officers of a certain corps that some-where in their neighborhood was a missionary who, as they sup-posed, would be able to give them desirable information, and per-haps assistance. They had seen certain natives wearing crosses, and when questioned they were found to know a few words of Latin; such words as *Christus* and *Maria.* It was possible that this missionary might be Spanish or even Portuguese, yet most prob-able that he would be a Frenchman; so the officers decided to seek him out, and the next day three of them with an escort ar-rived at his village.

What Père Loraine's feelings were when he first heard the voices of his own countrymen speaking the language of his youth, those will know best who have experienced the same. Indeed, it is only in foreign lands that all the music of our native speech comes home to us. What old scenes can it not evoke! Everything so long forgotten comes back as we listen, and in an instant we are home again with Youth and Beauty and High Aspiration.

What the result of this French invasion would be, whether good or ill, was not now to be considered, and in any case noth-ing could be altered; so, while the natives regarded their teacher wonderingly, he poured forth the history of his twenty years' exile to his countrymen. Yesterday it did not seem that he had any in-terest in any kingdom save God's, but now, most eagerly, his ears drank in the news from *la patrie.* Nay, but he asked for news of his mother and his friend. Alas! he had thought—but of course they could not know. And so they talked, forgetting their surroundings and the cause of their meeting; but when the past had been told over they began to consider the present, and the officers made known why they had come to him: could he, Père Loraine, help them with guides, interpreters, and maps? And they left him to consider it. His natural impulse was to comply with their wish, and aid them to the extent of his power with his maps. See! they would be of use at last; and with his advice, telling them all that his long experience had discovered—hold! would not this be the act of a traitor? Verily it would be like delivering the keys of a castle to its enemies—these keys which he had obtained by subterfuge.

This subterfuge had been justifiable, he believed, by the end for which, till now, he had used it; but would he be honest if he used weapons so obtained for anything short of this end? Was the welfare of his fatherland a sufficient excuse for him if he gave over the keys or the maps to these officers? He hesitated till morning; but when the officers came he had decided.

Yes, he would help them. It might be wrong—he feared it was; and yet with or without his help the result would be the same; namely, the French would take Tonquin, and his resistance would retard them but little. Yes, here were his maps, and old Mot-Ba, there, would serve as a guide and interpreter, and—God speed to them!

For these they thanked him and went their ways.

As in a dream Père Loraine goes apart into a little room, and all day long he sits there thinking of what he has done; but thinking most, I ween, of his lost youth, which is all back again so suddenly. Had he been wise? Would it not have been better if he had remained in Paris and withstood the temptations to a life of luxury? Ah, things looked so different now!

Perhaps self had led him to Tonquin, and not alone God's voice; perhaps, after all, his life was a failure. O, in very much he knew it was a failure, and this was a bitter thought. What were the few converts he had made here compared to the thousands he could have turned to God in Paris? Nay, but surely God's voice had called him to this particular work; he had heard it so plainly, again and again. . . . Had he? Had it really been God's voice—or his own wish? *Had he not heard what he wanted to hear?* "My God, my God, why hast thou forsaken me?" and in an agony of soul he drops on his knees. . . .

There is a tumult without: natives in a rage running to and fro. What was this their teacher had done? Sold their country? Given maps and a guide to the enemy? Ha, the traitor! for this he had come to them; they could see now that he was a Frenchman himself and no Annamite. So he had come beforehand; he had sneaked in among them to learn their ways and their language, all, all, in order to betray them. And in a blind fury they dashed into the little room where the priest was still kneeling; and there, before his crucifix, they beat him down and with heavy knives hacked off his head.

HOMESICKNESS

"East, West,
Home's best."

Hugo,—that was what we called him,—Hugo Heilmann; but it was generally understood that this was only a *nom de guerre.* His real name, whatever it may have been, was well known in the Swiss canton from which he had come; for there one of his uncles was a bishop of the church, and another was a dignitary of state.

Hugo was only a boy when he began to read books of travel, and his favorite study was always geography.

His childhood was passed with his mother and some servants on the side of a mountain, with the view enclosed by other mountains, and it was this feeling of being shut in that first put thoughts of wandering in his head. He must see beyond; he must get out of his cage.

His mother, poor woman, had thought to keep him there, all to herself; but seeing how restless he became, she resolved to send him away to school.

The bishop was consulted, and soon Hugo had exchanged one cage for another.

The mountains had shut him in from the rest of the world, yet he could climb to the tops of some of them and look out of a window, so to say; but here, inside the walls of this grim religious school, he began to stifle. Now, however, he could read and hear of the outside world; so he waited. Something would happen by and by, and meanwhile he studied geography,—other things too; and good reports of him were sent to his mother in the mountains.

But the something he waited for did not happen.

"I must make it happen," he thought; and so one Sunday he climbed over the high wall, and wandered at will through the town. There was music and dancing, and these amused him for a time; then as he turned away, a scout from the school came by, and taking his arm marched him back to his cage. He had broken the rule, so he must be punished; he must be locked in his own room for a week.

Two days he endured it, and then he asked to see the master.

"Please let me out," he said, "and I will not climb over the wall again."

"Your punishment will end on Sunday," said the master; "but if you are quiet and obedient you may be set free on Saturday."

By Saturday Hugo was in Paris. To make ropes of his bed-sheets and climb out of his window was a very simple matter. Others had done the same thing, why should not he?

He had some money and a watch, and other objects of value, so to buy a ticket and ride to Paris was also a simple matter. It seemed a great thing to Hugo, and he was in a fever of excitement and expectation all the way.

Both his uncles and his mother came in search of him, but they were too late; he had enlisted as a soldier in the Foreign Legion, and was over in Algeria before they reached Paris. He was indeed only eighteen years old, but being strong and well developed, he was believed when he claimed to be older.

"From bad to worse" is the commonest law of nature, and Hugo soon found that his condition was not improved. He had sought freedom, and he had found a heavy bondage. Truly he was seeing the world; seeing strange scenes and strange people, but all through the bars of his prison window. The restraint he had felt at home and at school was feather-light compared with the oppressing influence he was now subject to. Already he contemplated escape. So it is: we make our bed all of rose-leaves, as we suppose, but find it full of thorns and broken glass—and of scorpions, it may be. Must we perforce still lie in it?

Hugo was no way inclined to make the best of it; the pleasure of seeing the world, on which he had staked everything, was gone; he felt only the thorns in his bed, and could think only of how to escape from them. Why not run away? He had run away from school very successfully—he would try it again. He waited only for a chance. "But there is no use in waiting for what may never come; so much I have learned; I will make a chance," he thought, and so the next day he was far from his regiment, walking along a broad, white road towards the city of Oran. Hunger and thirst began to attack him, but they could not make him forget that now, at last, he was free.

It was a great sense of liberty which filled his mind, and he would think of nothing else. At last he had his desire; and with joy in his heart he went along, singing and dancing over the dusty highway. Then all at once he stood still, for he heard the noise of galloping horses coming behind him.

Peering through some bushes behind which he had hastily hid, he saw two officers riding past.

He lay still for a long time, then he began to tremble; all his sense of freedom was gone, and his mind was filled with new emotions. Where was he going? What was he to do? How could he find food? The Future, grim of aspect, stood sphinx-like before him.

"I must get out of Algeria," he thought, "away from French possessions. I'll make my way somehow into Spain." Hereupon he fell asleep and dreamed of the Alhambra. It was dark night when he awoke, and he felt great thirst. For an instant he could not remember what had happened, and when it all came before his mind he shuddered.

He started on his way, but looking up at the stars he found he was going back instead of forward.

Quickly he retraced his steps, and hearing the barking of dogs, he was aware that a village—at least a habitation—must be near.

As the moon came up, he saw, to the right, the dark outline of an Arab's tent. "Good!" he said. "Now I will test the much-talked-of hospitality of the Arabs," and boldly he approached the tent. "If these Arabs had met me on the road they would have brought me back to my regiment and claimed a reward, but if I come to them as a guest they must treat me as a friend."

And so it was: not bread and water alone he was given, but goats' milk, with dates and Koos-Koos. Then on sheepskins he slept till morning; but before his hosts were awake he arose and stole away, even as they had warned him to do.

Many days and nights did Hugo wander about, now losing, now finding his way; sometimes living on unripe fruit, and sometimes fed by the Arabs or by Spanish farmers. Eventually he reached a seaport and was wondering how he could cross to Spain, when the question was decided by a member of the city police, who took him in charge and had him sent back under escort to his regiment. A deserter? No; but he must be punished for "illegal absence from his corps." Moreover, as it was found that he had lost part of his equipment he must be court-martialed. Two years in the penitentiary was the verdict.

Alas, and had it come to this? Were all his dreams of freedom to end thus in prison? Nay,

> "Stone walls do not a prison make,
> Nor iron bars a cage."

This is a fine thought, to be sure; but then Hugo did not think it.

While waiting for his trial he had read on the walls of his cell many wise maxims: "Misery does not exist for the philosopher."—"The door of death is not locked."—"A thousand years from now, what will it matter?" *et cetera.*

He read them all over and over, and day after day; but he saw no meaning in them: they did not seem to apply to his case. Of course he had been foolish, but surely he had done no great evil that he must be so greatly punished. He had only wanted liberty, and had always found captivity. Why was it? This was the question which troubled him, and he could find no answer to it. Perhaps it was all to teach him the lesson of patience. Patience! this virtue of the dumb animals—why should it be so necessary for us? Why must we fold our hands and wait?—Why?

"Pshaw!" said Hugo; "I cannot understand it. I would gladly resist, but I find I must submit."

Thus in bitterness and silence his two years were passed. . . . After that they sent him to our regiment, then stationed at Tiaret, to finish his military service; and there I came to know him.

Why he made a confidant of me I do not know. I did not like him in the least, but seeing how unhappy he was, I listened to him patiently, and showed him a half-hearted sympathy—almost more than I really felt. "What is it you most regret?" I asked him.

"I regret everything. All my time is passed in thinking: if I had not done this! If I had not said that! And the knowledge that those things cannot be undone is my one grief."

"You had much better forget all about it, and make up your mind to do your duty now as well as possible. You have failed in your duty to your mother and to your school-master; now your duty is to France. You must try to be a clean, obedient soldier. It is not too late to start on a better road; you are still young." But nothing I could say ever seemed to take hold of him. "You must look forward," I continued. "Think of the joy of returning to your mountains. At your age you have no right to despair. Some day you will go home, and all you are now going through will be like a dream: you will wonder if it really took place in your life. The fact that nothing—neither misery nor joy—is of long duration should teach us submission."

"O, I see you will teach me philosophy," he returned; "I have read it all on my prison walls. But is it true? Do you feel it yourself? Can you stifle present pain by contemplating the time when it will be past? Can you?"

"No, I can not," I answered. "Misery is a reality for me, and I am afraid it always will be. But sometimes I can laugh at it; sometimes I can put it aside. Otherwise. . . . Can you not remember George Dandin? It is perhaps a poor comfort to think how we have made our own misfortune; yet there is a certain grim satisfaction in *paying our scot*, in bearing the results of our foolishness. If you will only cultivate a sense of the ridiculous you will find pleasure where now you find sorrow."

"Is that your plan?" he asked. "Do you succeed in it?"

"Please leave me out of the question," I answered. "I know what I say is true; it does not matter whether I act on it or not."

Poor Hugo! He tried bravely to be patient, but I could see that he suffered a great deal. I wondered whether he would ever look cheerful. One day he came to me with a light of hope in his face. "Do you know? I am going to Tonquin; and I shall desert again at Port Saïd or at Singapore, as it may turn out."

"If you will take my advice," I began; but remembering that no one takes advice which does not correspond with his own wishes, I broke off and started again.

"Have you looked at all sides of the question?" I asked.

"No; I have considered nothing but the success of my plan. I suppose if I should fail in it, I would be worse off than ever; but I shall succeed."

"Well, and if you do, if you manage to get free of the ship, what will you do in a strange country, without friends and without money?"

"O, I will be free! I will go and come at my pleasure."

"Yes; till you are arrested for vagabondage."

He looked a little rebuffed at this, but his new idea was not to be lightly shaken. "I shall try it, anyway," he said; "and if I fail— why, *'The door of death is not locked,'*" and he smiled sadly.

"I need not tell you that you are a fool, since you know it, and you will not thank me for any advice; but tell me, you have lived this life three years: can you not endure the rest of it? It will not kill you, and later on you will see much that was delightful in it. You will have forgotten all the fatigues and annoyances, and will call to mind how soundly you slept after a long march. You will remember your strong, healthy appetite, which made the rough food so good.

"Then your heart will beat faster as you think of the affectionate brotherhood which existed between you and your comrades; you will have forgotten their names, perhaps, but their faces will come before you often and often, and you will ask yourself if you were really unhappy in this life."

But Hugo was not heeding me; he was thinking of other things. He was at home, and he saw visions.

He saw a large Swiss châlet built against a mountain, with heavy stones holding down the roof. He saw his mother sitting out on the veranda waiting. The cherry-tree, all in bloom, cast flickering shadows here and there as the wind played in its branches; showers of white petals flew circling through the air, and some of them fell at his mother's feet. "She does not feel them," he thought; "but if my lips could touch her feet, then she would feel."

And he saw the swallows flying in and out at the eaves, and he thought: "They bring her no message from me; she does not heed them; but when I return she will not sit still; then this look of sorrow will leave her face." . . .

Hugo caught my hand. "You don't know," he sobbed. "How

can you know what I suffer? I am homesick. Do you know what that is? I cannot wait, I must go home. Every day is as a year. I count the days; I count the hours. You say this is childish, that I am a fool; you are right, but I cannot help it. I try hard to forget my home, but every incident reminds me of it. I try in vain to overcome this feeling and I am utterly unhappy."

"But at least you have not lost your reason," I said; "you can still consider the matter logically. See: you want to go home as soon as possible, but you are determined to do something which, nine chances out of ten, will defer your return indefinitely. This is not wise. Have you learned nothing from your past experience?"

"It is you who will not understand!" he cried. "How can a man who is dying of thirst hold back his hand when a cup is held out to him? The cup may contain poison, you say. And what of it? he is dying anyway. Also, there is a chance that it may contain water. O, I will not, I cannot wait! I will do as I say; and if I fail, I will give up the struggle."

And so Hugo went to Tonquin. . . .

I often asked for news of him, whether he had deserted at Port Saïd or at Singapore, but no one could tell me.

I hoped he might have succeeded, and whenever I remembered him I pictured him at home with his mother. . . .

Our transport reached Tonquin in May, and at once we were sent on up the Red River to our respective posts.

As we passed through the other posts along the route we were greeted with enthusiasm by the old comrades, many of whom we had known in Algeria. In particular were we well received at Cham-Khé: every one, men and officers, came out to welcome us. No, not every one, either; for as we were shown into a large *cania* where we were to pass the night, I saw a soldier sitting apart in a corner. Something in his attitude looked familiar, and after I had arranged my effects I walked towards him. "Why, it is Hugo!" I cried. "Halloo! have you forgotten your friends?" and I went over and touched him. By an effort he pulled himself together and wished me a cold welcome.

Then he sank back into thought—or into an absence of thought.

"What is the matter?" I asked. "Are you ill?"

"No,—yes,—I don't know." And then he made another effort and regained something of his old manner.

"You did not succeed?" I questioned. "You did not manage to get away at Singapore?"

"No; I did not try. I might have done it, but I saw my mother, and she bade me not to attempt it."

"You saw your mother? Where? How?"

"O, I saw her while I was asleep. Do you laugh?"

"No; why should I laugh?"

"But I have not seen her since, and I fear"—and here he paused and said no more.

"What's the matter with Hugo?" I asked of Müller, who came up to greet me. "He has not had a sunstroke, has he? Or has he taken to drink?"

"O, no, nothing of that; he is always the same. I don't know— nobody knows what ails him. He never speaks unless we speak to him first, and he does nothing but sit and mope. We have tried to shake him out of it, but you see how he is. Now we just let him alone."

The next morning, before we continued our journey I talked again with Hugo.

"As far as I have heard and read you are taking the right way to fall a victim to this climate. I don't suppose your life is of much value to yourself, but you should not forget that your mother is waiting for you to return. For her sake you must come out of your melancholia. You should be a man; you must not act like a boy."

"O, I know all that," he replied; "but you see there is no hope in my life. I will soon know—I fear my mother is dead; but I have written home to one of my school-fellows for news; I expect his letter soon. I shall keep up till then, till I know for certain."

"Well, and if it is as you fear?"

"O, then— 'The door of death is not locked,' and who knows what will happen?"

"Look here, Hugo, I've something for you. You used to be interested in the study of geography. Have you ever tried astronomy? Here in my *sac* is one of Flammarion's most interesting books, 'The Plurality of Inhabited Worlds.'"

A little light was in his eyes as I began to speak, but it soon faded.

"O, thank you, but I know all Flammarion's books. Astronomy, that is to say the stars, are too far away; we can only theorize about them."

"Have you tried to learn the Annamite language?" I asked.

"No; but it is bread I desire, and you offer me stones. I ask for my home, and you send me to the stars, or you bid me remain in Tonquin. I tell you I cannot forget."

"Well, here is another thought for you, then. You think, you are sure, that you would be happy if you were at home; but you ought to know that happiness is not attached to any particular place in the world. We have happiness in ourselves, or, as is most often the case, we do not have it at all. Of course, certain conditions, certain outward circumstances, may augment or diminish our happiness, but they cannot create it.

"Let us suppose that you were to go home to-morrow: you believe that one sight of your mountains would put all your sadness to flight. Perhaps it might; but in a few days your sadness would return, and you would ask, 'Is this all? Is this what I desired so much?' Then your discontent would return, and you would recall with regret all these scenes which now you seem to ignore.

"Be sure that if ever you are to find happiness in this world, you must not seek it outside of your own heart. Plant seeds of contentment, and happiness will grow from them."

"Yes, you were always free with advice; nay, I see, too, the force of your words, but they all fall dead before my misery."

"Well, here is still another thought for you. From all I have read, added to what I have felt, I believe that the love of one thing may make us indifferent to another; so it would be wise for you to learn to love something or some one here present, rather than to break your heart longing for what is far away."

"O, 'words are indeed the physicians of a distempered feeling,'—you remember the quotation; but I ask you with Job,—who was also a wise man,—'What doth your arguing reprove?'"

"Good-by, then," I said; "I must go. We are to be at Yen-Luong; will you send me a letter now and then?"

"Perhaps,—or no; I had better not promise. Good-by!"

We had been at Yen-Luong for a few weeks when one day the *dramh,* that is to say, the letter-carrier, brought me a letter from Hugo.

"Because you desire my happiness," he wrote, "I will you that I am now happier than you can well imagine. You remember I wrote to my comrade, asking him to send me news of my mother, and desiring him to keep silent about having heard from me. He at once brought my letter to my mother, and she has written to me, so kind, so good a letter. You cannot know how happy it has made me, and how doubly miserable at the same time. Never has my desire for home been as ardent as it is now. How can I endure to wait, now that I know my mother has forgiven me! I pray you write to me. I will try to be patient; there is no other means of being at peace—no other means, except . . . Adieu!"

The day I received this letter I was sent elsewhere with an escort, so I put off answering it till I should return. But when I came back I no longer thought of it. I was sure to see him later on, so I let it go, and after another week I heard from him again.

I was fast asleep one hot afternoon when Kautor came in and shook me by the shoulder. "O, what do you want?" I grumbled; "I wish you would go"—but looking in his face I changed my sentence, "What is it?"

"Hugo is dead. You know Hugo Heilmann, at Cham-Khé. He left a letter for you here"—

"Did he kill himself?" I asked.

"Yes."

I took the letter and went down to the pagoda in the bamboo grove to read it in peace.

It was very short: "Adieu, dear friend! I cannot bear it any longer; but *'the door of death is not locked!'*—HUGO."

SLOVATSKI

By sickness and death our company had lost a large number of men, and those of us who remained had double duty to perform.

It is stipulated that soldiers shall sleep six nights out of seven, yet if we spent two nights a week in bed we were fortunate.

The result of this was more sickness and more death, till we lost courage and even ceased to grumble.

What was the use? Perhaps we too would fall sick, and then we would be sure of a rest,—at the hospital or in the cemetery. The outlook was grim, but anything would be better than this struggle.

When seen of men and approved, it is pleasant to act bravely and to sacrifice one's self; but when your officers ignore everything but their own well-being, and take your best service for granted, then the strain seems futile, and despair and slack service may result.

At last we heard good news: a transport ship was bringing a large reënforcement of *Légionnaires,* and all the posts on the Red River were to be strengthened.

How eagerly we waited, making an extra effort, stimulated by the hope of better times!

A great amusement was to speculate as to who would come; whether any of the old comrades from Saïda would be sent to our post. We longed for something—anything that would recall the past; so, even Gofin would have been welcomed with delight, though at Saïda we had ignored him—poor old Gofin, the scapegrace of the regiment! But there were Lenoir, and Casanova, and Denkwitz, and scores of others who might come,—what a welcome we would give them! For me, I was in a high state of jubilation: the last letter I had received from Herx told me that he was sure to come with the next transport. This was the glad thing for me to think about. Herx, who spoke such exquisite German; whose voice made harsh gutturals more soft and sweet than all the Italian vowels; and when he repeated Heine's songs—ah, there never was such music! If only he would be sent to our post,—that was the doubt which kept me subdued.

But at any rate I would meet him, and our correspondence would continue less brokenly.

I had never seen Herx but once; we had been thrown together for a day, but as water joins with water, so had we rushed together in a marvellous reciprocity of thought and sentiment.

A year after he had learned my address, and since then our letters had been as frequent as possible. He did not say so, but I knew it was mostly the hope of meeting me that was bringing him to Tonquin, and so I waited for him eagerly. . . . But no, he did not come—not to our post, at least; he had been sent off to Tuyen-Quanh from Ha-Noï, where the detachment had separated. Those who arrived at our post were all strangers to us. As they marched in we watched them in silence and dismay; not a face was familiar. They were for the most part young men, and how would they stand the service? Pshaw! we would soon be as badly off as ever, for these fellows would be down with fever before a week could pass.

There were three new men for our squad, and one of them was given a bed next to mine; his name was Slovatski, and he was a Russian; but as I looked at him my heart stopped beating. "Good Lord!" I cried in English, "don't you know me?" For as I believed there was my old friend Leonard, whom I had known years before.

Slovatski looked at me blankly, just as Leonard would have done, then slowly he smiled and said in German: "You speak English, but I do not know what you say."

Of course it was impossible that this could be Leonard, but a more exact resemblance I had never seen. I explained this to Slovatski, and laughing over it we became friendly.

"Did you know any one on shipboard named Herx?" I asked.

"Herx? Was he a Rhinelander with a white beard and blue eyes?"

"Yes, he was a Rhinelander," I said; "but I don't remember that he had a beard—or—yes; that must have been he. Do you know where he has been sent?"

"To Tuyen-Quanh, I think, but I'm not sure; he may have stopped at Son-Tay. I get these outlandish places mixed up. I don't know yet what you call this post."

"O, this is Trai-Hut," I said, "one of the worst posts on the river; if you could have stopped at Kam-Khé, or even at Yen-Luong, you would have fared better. We used to be at Yen-Luong, but we came up here a few months ago."

The longer I talked with Slovatski, the more I was struck by his resemblance to Leonard. It was not merely in his face, but in his whole person: the shape of his hands, the drawling mode of speech; everything about him but the German tongue reminded me forcibly of the year I had spent with Leonard in the Connecticut Valley.

"How is it you don't speak English?" I asked. "All the Russians I ever knew before spoke English."

"Well, I never had a chance to learn it; but if you'll teach me I'll begin." This was not what I had expected and hardly what I wanted, so I gave him a half-hearted response.

"You remember when you first saw me, you thought you recognized me. How was it?" So I told him in detail of his strange resemblance to my old friend Leonard.

"What! he is an American! I look like an American? How do you account for it?"

"I don't account for it at all. I only tell you the fact, and leave you to account for it—or to forget it, as you like."

But Slovatski did not forget it, and we never talked for ten minutes together without his returning to the subject. "Do you say your friend was *just* like me? The same hair, the same everything?"

"All but the speech," I said. "If you were to speak English with the Connecticut accent the likeness would be perfect."

After that Slovatski stopped trying to learn English, and then another day he asked: "Did your friend wear a beard?"

"No; he only wore a moustache, just as you do." And after that Slovatski let his beard grow, and again he asked:

"Do I still look like your friend?"

"Yes," I said; "but if I had not seen you first without a beard I would not have noticed it, perhaps. But why? You seem to worry about it; there is nothing in it, only a chance resemblance."

"O, yes, there is something in it; nothing happens by chance. I don't want to resemble any one like that. One of us is enough in the world. Say, is your friend healthy? Is he strong? How old is he?"

"Why, Slovatski! what in the world ails you? What can it possibly matter to you that there is a man on the other side of the world who looks like you? There is not one chance in a million that you will ever see him." As I looked at Slovatski I saw that the mere thought of seeing Leonard made him turn pale. Well, what queer superstition was this? But, strangely enough, the more Slovatski tried to change his appearance, the more clearly did I see his resemblance to Leonard; but finding how it worried him I never alluded to it. Again and again as I have watched him I have waited to hear Leonard's voice with the well-remembered nasal twang, so when Slovatski spoke German with the Berlin accent I have started at the incongruity of it. He would notice this and say: "O, I see; you think now of your friend in America. I don't look like him now, do I?" . . .

Alas, no; the resemblance was fast disappearing: the ruddy cheeks were becoming thin and pale; the full, red lips were growing drawn and pinched; and the merry blue eyes were shaded by dark circles. So the likeness was fast going; only the expression of the eyes remained, and the same smile showed the same white teeth.

"What is the matter with you?" I asked. "Have you the fever? You look very much altered."

"I don't know what it is," he answered. "I suppose it is the climate,—and I am always thinking of Odessa; wishing I were back there."

"Odessa? Why, I thought you came from Moscow."

"O, no, my home is in Odessa. I was at school in Moscow, and many of my friends are there; that is why I talk about it."

"Well, I thought no one but Jews lived at Odessa; that was why I was surprised. You're not a Jew, are you?"

"No, not exactly; but I dare say some of my ancestors were Jews. You don't like them?"

"O, I'm not particular; a Jew or a Gentile, it is all one to me."

"What ever started you to talk about Jews, I wonder. With me it is a sore subject. I would not have been here but for them."

"No? How so?"

"It is hardly just to say that, either, I suppose. You see I wanted to marry a Jewess, and my father would not have it; so we had a quarrel instead of a wedding, and I ran away. Minka—her name was Minka—would not marry me without my father's consent, so I quarrelled with her too! That made me desperate; and being in Paris without any money, I enlisted in the Legion, like so many others. You are sure I don't look like your friend in America now?"

Thus it was: whatever we talked about he always came back to that old question. "No," I said; "not as you did when I first saw you. But what of it anyway? Why do you care?"

"I care, because I believe that if two look alike they are alike, and one of my kind is enough in the world. Do you see?"

"No, I don't see; or at least I see that you are what my friend in America would call a *crank*, which means as much or as little as you like."

This was my last talk with Slovatski. In the night I fell sick with some bad fever and was taken next day into the store-room, where I was expected to die. Fischer died, and two others of our squad, but I began to recover.

When they could move me I was taken down to the river and embarked in a Chinese junk. No sooner were we started southward than I began to feel strong and well, and my first impulse led me to stand up and see what was taking place.

Besides the coolies who were guiding the junk, I found that there were two other *Légionnaires* aboard—and one of them was Slovatski; he lay in a corner, and he was delirious.

I turned to the other, who was sitting up, and asked where we were going.

"Why, to the infirmary at Yen-Bay; that is, if you live till we get there."

"And you? Are you ill too?"

"No, I am going down to replace a fellow at Than-Ba."

"And is there no escort with us? Are we three alone with the coolies?"

"Yes, quite alone. Are you afraid of pirates?"

"No."

Then I crept over and looked at Slovatski; he was unconscious. I put my hand on his head and felt it to be hot, and his temples throbbed under my fingers. He was talking fast and furiously, but in a low tone. What he said was in Russian, but the word "Minka" recurring often, I supposed his ravings to be of the past.

"Is he going to die?" I asked of the other.

"Yes, it looks like it."

"Can't we do anything for him? Did the captain send no medicine with us?"

"No, there is nothing we can do that I know of. But how is it that you are better? You were worse than he when we started."

"I don't know; I suppose it is the motion of the junk that has revived me." Poor Slovatski! if only I could revive him! I got cold tea and hot wine for him, but could not arouse him from his sleep.

Alas, that we grow so selfish under suffering! I felt—I knew—that Slovatski was dying, and for my life I could not care much about it. So many had died; so many whom I had known and loved; and now one more was going, that was all. Yes, if I could have saved him by any possible means I would gladly have done it,—but how?

Since then I have thought of many things I might have tried, but at the time I thought only of cold tea and hot wine, and why either of them occurred to me I cannot now imagine; perhaps my head was still muddled from the fever. Poor Slovatski! his heavy breathing kept time with the noise of the poles with which the coolies guided the junk; and I lay down near him and listened.

As we approached Ngoï-Thie the night came on, and with it a chill wind; so I thought I would lend my blanket to Slovatski. As I wrapped it around his feet I heard him muttering in German. "What is it, Slovatski? What can I do for you?" I whispered.

"O, is it you?" he gasped. "Say, do I look like him now? I don't look like him now, do I?"

O, so eager was his question!

"No, O, no!" I cried; "you never looked like him; how could you? It was all a mistake. I only said—that you must forget it.

Here—here is some tea; you should like tea, being a Russian."

But before I could get it he began to rave again. I think he was repeating Russian poetry, for his words were measured and rhythmical. It may have been Pushkin's verses which he was reciting, if I had but known.

I lay down again and listened. I was cold without my blanket, but I knew Slovatski would not need it much longer, so I waited.

Presently the motion of the junk ceased, and on calling to the other fellow, I found that we had stopped for the night in front of Ngoï-Thie.

"Shall we go ashore?" I asked.

"No; we will be as safe and comfortable where we are," he said.

Slovatski went on breathing heavily, but with more and more difficulty; now that the noise of the boat's motion had ceased I could hear the "swish, swish" which his breath made in surging between his closed teeth. Sometimes it would miss, but only to begin again with more force.

I thought I would go to sleep for a while, feeling sure that the complete stopping of Slovatski's breathing would awaken me; I would know that to be the end, and—I could have my blanket again! I soon fell asleep, but with my mind full of Slovatski I began to dream of him.

I was still asleep, I suppose, but suddenly I grew conscious, as I thought, of some one leaning over Slovatski,—some one holding a lighted candle. Was it one of the coolies? for I saw long black hair hanging over to the floor; and then slowly the figure turned, and a white face, very beautiful, looked at me—a Jewish face! Aye, it was Minka! But when I sat up and rubbed my eyes, I saw nothing,—only Slovatski's white hand moving vaguely through the air.

The sound of his breathing was no longer audible, so I crept over to him and took his hand and listened. . . . "One in the world is enough," he said. "One of us is enough." And then something rattled in his throat, and Slovatski was dead.

I told the other fellow, but he only grumbled something, angry at being disturbed for such a trifle.

The coolies who were awake burned incense and sweet-smelling wood, while they murmured, "*Shim, shim Buddha, shim, shim Buddha,*" and I know not what else, all in a monotone. For me, I sat there quite still, thinking.

Slovatski's journey was over; but, alas! mine must continue; so gently I removed the blanket from his feet, and warmed by it I was soon asleep.

A SPIRITUAL COMBAT

We always called her "*Muoï*," which in the Annamite tongue means ten; and this name would indicate that she was the tenth daughter of her family, though, in fact, few Annamite families are so numerous. Muoï was theatrical; she had lived at Ha-Noï, where she had learned many wonderful things. The reason why she had left the Annamite stage was a secret, guessed to be an affair of the heart which she had had with a French officer, since dead. I dare say this rumor was true.

She always wore the finest and gayest of silk garments, of which she had somewhere and somehow gathered a great variety. At the time I speak of, Muoï was mistress to a civilian functionary in the Administration, but she had very loose rein, and ran about the place at her own good pleasure. She was no way beautiful, but she was always so bright and fresh looking, and had such soft, sweet manners, that we were always pleased to meet her; and then she had learned and adopted certain European customs which set her apart from the other *Kongois.* For instance, although she smoked cigarettes,—many European ladies do that,—she did not smoke the Annamite pipe, nor did she stain her lips by chewing *betel.* Neither were her pretty teeth covered with black enamel, as according to Annamite fashion they should have been. Probably the defunct French officer had been the chief factor in produc-ing such result. However, we all found that Muoï was charming, even though her nose was flat and her eyes were oblique. She learned to speak French fairly well, and it was amusing to hear her answer grammatically when we would address her in the jumble of "pigeon French" best understood by the natives. Her voice was not musical according to our ideas, but never have I heard a voice so soft and pleasing; and in this she was not unlike other Anna-mite women, whose tones are surprisingly agreeable to the ear: the poorest peasant woman scarcely speaks above a whisper, and always in a soft, purring, twittering way, suggestive of birds, yet without being strictly musical.

One day I went down to see Muoï's proprietor, and found him

fast asleep in a hammock, while she, at a little distance, was amusing herself with a sword exercise, which was a remembrance from her past theatrical experience. I held my breath; but she saw me, and glad perhaps of a spectator, continued with fresh vigor. Such a sight as it was! O, a sight to be remembered forever! Of course, I did not understand it, but as she went on, I fitted a meaning to it which seemed to apply aptly enough. I dare say the true original meaning was far other; but of true art—and this was the truest of art—who will restrict or limit the meanings? So much precision; such an exactitude of motion. Every gesture, every thrust, every stroke, every feint,—all had been learned with mechanical accuracy, and she now performed them with a vigor, a swiftness, a fire, a fury, which fascinated and dazzled me. But what did it mean? With what or whom was Muoï fencing? With a shadow? A spirit? Yes, so at least I understood it. She was warring with an evil spirit. Was it perhaps with the ghost of the French officer, her whilom lover? How her sword flew! O, she would win, I saw that, in the pride and courage flashing from her dark eyes! At times, after a heavy stroke, by which for an instant the evil spirit was beaten back, Muoï would toss her sword high in the air, spring and catch it as it fell, and then flourish it triumphantly, as if in an ecstasy of conscious superiority.

And then I wrongly thought the end had come. She redoubled her strokes, she made them heavier; there was no more play, no more flourishes; all was now serious, for the spirit must be vanquished. No trembling in the small right hand, no nervousness in any of her swift movements; and yet I caught my breath lest by a chance she should fail; for all idea that it was only play had left me, and her failure would have distressed me. Faster and faster flew her sword, till at last, with one great wheeling stroke, she seemed to win. Then with a wild laugh of triumph she cast her sword high in the air, nor did she try to catch it as it fell ringing to the floor.

As I said, I thought this was the end; but not so. After she had sat for an instant, gazing at the sword which lay at some distance from her, she started up, uttering a suppressed cry of terror. She seized the sword and recommenced the fight. But, whereas before all had been so exact and accurate, all was now hurried and nervous. Now, as her strokes fell on all sides, I seemed to understand it. Now it was no longer one shadow, one spirit with which she had to fight, but here was a horde of evil spirits. All the haunting memories, all the black shadows, all the dreadful ghosts from out her past life,—there they were, all of them, all in armor before her, all surging and raging madly against her. It was noon of an Asiatic summer day, yet I saw these ghosts distinctly, conjured in my mind as they were by the art of Muoï's movements.

Her sword, as she sent it circling through the air, might keep them off for a time; but the conflict, bravely and courageously as she fought it, was too unequal; no merely human force could prevail against that ghostly army. O, yes, she must fail; she knew it; but still she kept on, with a wild fear—the awful terror of death—visible in her ashy face. My excitement grew so great that I cried aloud, for, following so closely with my eyes the strokes she made, I became gradually conscious that her chief effort was made against one of these spirits, the one who was boldest and strongest of the throng; and to whom I gave the name of *Remorse.* Ah! let her but slay him, so I thought, and all the others will fly off. But, alas! she lost hope; she knew she must fail, and the knowledge of it unnerved her arm, and made her movements uncertain and faltering. Then came the end; her long, black hair became unfastened from the *baba* in which it had been twisted, and fell in thick, straight locks down to her knees; this, blinding her, and checking her blow, ended the fray. She threw back her hair with her left arm, and stood for an instant quite unguarded. Then the sword of *Remorse* struck in and pierced her to the heart. She shrieked out a great sobbing cry, dropped her sword, flung wide her arms, and fell forward on her face.

In a minute she jumped to her feet, and, with a laugh at my excited expression, went and picked up her sword. She was pleased to have interested me, and seemed grateful when I complimented her. She asked me if I thought the ladies of France could act like that; whereupon I assured her that the "divine Sara" herself was not equal to anything like it; but Muoï had probably never heard Sara's name before, so she did not appreciate the extravagance of my praise.

And then I came away, for I had forgotten what I had come to say to Muoï's proprietor.

THE STORY OF YOUP-YOUP

It was in the year 1884, and already Youp-Youp was past the prime of life. She was a Kongoï, that is, an Annamite woman; but she was frequently called *baïa*, which means "old woman." She was one of the poor people; her ancestors had all been coolies, and she herself had been a cooly; but now, on certain days of the week, she would sit with her gossips in the market-place to sell the produce of a small garden, in which she worked on the other days; she toiled with patient industry, yet the few *sapiques* which she gained were scarcely sufficient to pay for the rice she ate.

Perhaps, counting by time rather than sorrows, Youp-Youp had not yet lived forty years; but gray hair, wrinkles, bent form, and palsied movements seemed to declare that she had lived for ages and ages. Such teeth as she had were covered with black enamel, and the habit of chewing *betel* did not improve her appearance; her eyes had, perhaps, never been very large, but now they were so concealed by wrinkles that unless she were astonished or frightened, they never became visible. Youp-Youp is what she was called, but in her youth this name may have been modified or extended by family or surname. I do not know about that.

Now, though she was a person of so small estate, of such insignificance, the story of her last days is not without interest, and so I will tell it as I interpreted from the scraps of it which came to my ears.

Perhaps I ascribe motives to Youp-Youp which never moved her; possibly the last six years have altered her story, and the facts of it may have been quite different from the present account; but I will give its details, which are not untrue to human nature— human nature which finds like expressions throughout the world—in Pekin as in Paris.

Youp-Youp lived at Ngoï-Lao, a pleasant village on the left bank of the Red River, a few days' journey north from Ha-Noï. The *cania* (bamboo cabin) which she occupied was clean to see, and the small garden behind it was managed with provident foresight: before one crop was reaped, another would be all ready to replace it; now cucumbers, anon tomatoes, and salad all the year round.

Youp-Youp had long outlived her family; one by one her husband and children had been taken hence by cholera, and in sign of mourning, the *baba,* or turban, which she wore on her head was white instead of black. I suppose she often wondered why she was left to such a cheerless life in this world, why she lived on after all whom she had loved and lived for were taken. When the past holds few joys, and the future offers small hopes, it requires much courage and endurance to live; still, Youp-Youp lived on like that till the year 1884, and then her life became eventful.

At the village of Ngoï-Lao it was told by one to another that the French were coming,—the French, who had taken all the chief cities of Tonquin, were now, in this year of 1884, laying hold of the towns and villages, and would soon be at Ngoï-Lao. One of the most effectual means of opposition practised by the Annamites in small places was to poison the wells, burn the *canias,* and having destroyed all the provisions which they could not carry, to run away into the mountains, whither the French could not follow them. This indeed was a negative sort of opposition, yet it retarded movements and increased the difficulty of the French invasion. This was the course which the villagers of Ngoï-Lao proceeded to adopt. Youp-Youp was told of the threatened danger, and invited to go to the mountains with her neighbors; but she chose to remain—to remain and take her chances with the French. After all, the French could only kill her, and she might as well die at home as in the mountains. No one tried to dissuade her, for in questions of personal safety little thought is given to the whims of an old woman; so when all her neighbors had fled, Youp-Youp sat alone in her house and waited. Whether she prayed to Buddha and made him offerings, or whether the habits and labors of her life had left her brain too dull to think about abstract subjects, is all matter which may go unanswered. The fact is, that next morning, when a large detachment of French soldiers arrived at Ngoï-Lao, Youp-Youp was their most unselfish benefactress. They came worn out by fatigue and hunger, wounds and sickness; and if Youp-Youp had not been there to render aid, few of them

had ever gone much farther. When she found out that they did
not kill her, as she expected,—perhaps hoped,—she at once
evinced her willingness and ability to help them. She got clean
mats for them to lie on, she showed them the one well which had
not been poisoned, she dressed their wounds, she gave them her
rice,—all she had,—and when they would return her any signs of
thankfulness, she would wrinkle up her face and whisper, "*Oo-tia!
Linh-tap flançais tot-lam, tot-lam!*" (Well! well! French soldiers
very good, very good!)

Time passed, and the story of Youp-Youp's ministrations to the
French became known and talked of in high places, and the result
of the talk was that the French government awarded the military
medal to Youp-Youp,—a decoration which entitles the owner to
an annual income of a few francs. I do not suppose Youp-Youp
ever understood it, but now, with the medal and the pension,
she found herself to have become an important personage in the
land. Ngoï-Lao was in a favorable position, and the French, seeing
this, lost no time in establishing a military post there; so in a few
months the village was rebuilt, and Annamites who had made
peace with the French came from other parts to live there; even
some of its old inhabitants came back from the mountains, and
these were certainly surprised to find Youp-Youp still alive and
even prosperous.

Now, you will remember that Youp-Youp belonged to the class
from which coolies are taken, that she had been a cooly herself,
and albeit that she still shut her eyes and whispered, "*Linh-tap
flançais tot-lam, tot-lam!*" she must often have had a different idea
when she saw how the "*linh-tap flançais*" treated the coolies. Did
she never say to herself, "*Linh-tap flançais tsou-lam, tsou-lam*"?
(French soldier very bad.)

The Frenchman, sick and worn with fatigue, is quite a tender-
hearted person compared with the Frenchman healthy and in
power. Well, but the French had paid her for her kindness, and
purchased her favor; and at first it was with a childish pleasure,
almost like happiness, that she wore her military medal. In sooth,
it looked out of place, pinned to her coarse brown tunic; yet she
wore it always at first, as I said, with pleasure, but afterwards

with shame and chagrin. Of course, it was jealousy alone which made Youp-Youp's neighbors resent her present fortune; but they made it appear to her, by daily word and innuendo, that by having helped the French, she had helped the oppressors of her people; she, whose fathers and forefathers had been coolies, had taken sides with their masters. And so shame and regret were on the underside of her life, though she still continued to whisper, "*Linh-tap flançais tot-lam, tot-lam!*"

Farther up the river was another village, larger and more prosperous than Ngoï-Lao. Youp-Youp had once been there in her youth, and still had a remembrance of the large market-place and the great pagoda.

One day it came to the ears of her understanding that the French were going up to take possession of this village, and the villagers had not been warned of it. This time it was intended that they should not have time to run away to the mountains. Here is what followed: the morning when the French arrived at the village gate, the form of an old Annamite woman was seen crouching before it. The sun had not arisen, and in the obscurity she was not recognized. They ordered her to open the gate, or to get aside out of the way; she did neither, and so some one thrust his bayonet into her back and shoved her from the gate. She did not cry out; she wrinkled up her face, and whispered for the last time, "*Oo-tia! Linh-tap flançais tot-lam, tot—!*"

But again she struggled to her knees, and tore something from the breast of her tunic and threw it from her as though it were a coal of fire; it was the military medal, for you see already that this was poor, sad-hearted old Youp-Youp whom they had killed. No one knew what she was doing there; she had been seen at Ngoï-Lao the day before, and to have come so far she must have walked all night long.

What I like to think is that she had come with the intention of warning the villagers of their danger, but worn out with fatigue, she had been unable to open the gate and accomplish her purpose.

ECKERMANN AND TANNEMEYER

What the secret between these two men may have been will never be known. I could not even find a plausible theory for their actions. They came together for the first time in their lives (so much my research seemed to prove) on the French transport ship "Colombo," out from Oran with soldiers for Tonquin. They came from different regiments of the Foreign Legion, and by some mistake they were quartered near each other on the ship; still, never was any acquaintance formed between them. With the rest of us they were both friendly and pleasant companions, but towards each other they were silent and unconscious; so much so that I and some others began to speak of it. Why did they ignore each other, we asked; for come to question them separately about themselves, we learned that they were both from the same city in Bavaria.

Then we supposed they were members of some secret society, the incomprehensible rules of which they were observing. So we laid traps for them, that we might discover if this were the case; but no, not at all. In the course of a week I became very friendly with each of them, and tried several times to bring them together in conversation; but I never succeeded. Anon, by quoting the sayings of one to the other I hoped to arouse their curiosity in each other. They were both musical, and from Tannemeyer I learned a number of Bavarian folk-songs. Speaking of these to Eckermann, his interest flamed up, and eagerly he asked me if I knew any more, and where I had learned them. "Why, I learned them from Tannemeyer," I said. "He has a long repertoire of them." Hearing this, Eckermann became as cold as a fish, and took no further interest in Bavarian folk-songs.

Tannemeyer was constantly trying to sketch; he had a passionate longing to learn how to draw, and pencil and paper were never long out of his hands; but for all his effort there was ever something wrong with his drawings. He knew it and sighed.

Then one day while I talked with Eckermann, he took from his pocket a small notebook to illustrate the point in question; a quick stroke or two of his pencil showed me that he was a clever draughtsman.

"Hallo!" I said, "where did you learn to draw?"

"At Munich," he answered. "Why?"

"O, nothing much; but will you lend me your note-book?" I saw it was nearly full of very beautiful drawings.

"Well," he said, "my sketches are not for show, and I have some things written in my note-book, so I"—

"But I will not show your book to any one, except to two or three of my friends. Nor shall I or any one read a word of it." I felt as if I were playing him a trick, for I saw he did not suspect that one of my "friends" was Tannemeyer.

Still I must see whether these drawings would leave Tannemeyer as cold as the folk-songs had left Eckermann. It was quite the same.

At first Tannemeyer glowed with enthusiasm. Had I made these sketches? and would I lend him the book to copy them? and would I teach him how to draw?

"But these are not mine," I said. "I could not make a line of them."

"Whose, then? Whose are they?" he exclaimed.

"They are Eckermann's," I answered, as naturally as I could.

"O," he said, and handed me back the note-book.

"But I am sure," I went on, "that he will be glad to lend you his book, or to give you lessons; he is a genuine good fellow is Eckermann. By the way, why do you never talk to him? He comes from your country; you'd be sure to find him very amusing."

"O, thank you; you are very kind; but please give him his note-book, and do not say you showed it to me."

"But why? Why not?" I insisted; "What in the name of commonsense is the matter with you two, that you must treat each other in this absurd way?"

I saw I had pained him by my question, and I began to apologize, but he hushed me up saying:

"Really I do not know in the least what it is that is between us; I have tried already to overcome it, but I could not. One cannot mix oil and vinegar, you know,—perhaps we are like that."

"But have you never spoken with each other? Have you never tried to overcome this antipathy?"

"My dear man, there is no antipathy, as you call it; it is not that, nor is it any lack of sympathy, either. I tell you again I do not know what it is. Whenever I try to analyze my feelings for Eckermann, I grow faint, I begin to shudder; in fact, I cannot fix my thoughts on him for any length of time. Never have I spoken to him, nor he to me; and never have I spoken of him before. If you will oblige me, please do not let us mention him again."

"But—well, forgive me, I have been indiscreet. I see it. Still, my reasons were neither selfish nor idle. I simply wanted to bring two good fellows together, that they might find the time less heavy. Will you forgive me?"

"O, certainly," he cried; "it is rather I who should claim your forgiveness for my unreasonable whim, as it must appear to you."

"Not at all," I expostulated. "I can quite understand that it is no fault of the oil that it cannot mix with the vinegar, and if I have failed to find a vehicle, I must eat my salad without a dressing, that is all. But," regretfully, "I would have delighted in having brought you two together. I am sure the conjunction would have been delectable for the rest of us."

I do not think Tannemeyer understood me; he stared blankly, and sauntered away.

The ship sailed on.

At Obok—or was it Aden?—we stopped to take on coal, and some of the natives came on board to sell fruit and other merchandise; but owing to a lack of money among us, the commerce was slow. We had nothing but our pay usually, and that hardly sufficed to furnish tobacco.

Latterly I had lost interest in the mystery of Eckermann and Tannemeyer, or rather my attention had been given elsewhere and I had not thought about them. Now, among these venders of fruit three fakirs had come on board, bringing charmed snakes and other odds and ends of their profession. With these they sat in a corner of the deck and began to juggle.

In their strange raiment and with their dramatic gestures they formed a picturesque group.

A crowd soon circled around them; I appeared late and had to remain on the outskirts of it, but there I saw what was more interesting to me than all the tricks of the snakes and the fakirs: there was Eckermann rapidly making a sketch of the group, and at two steps behind him stood Tannemeyer gazing over his shoulder with his soul in his eyes; he was trembling, and his fingers clasped and unclasped. I thought at first he was looking at the snakes; but no, it was at Eckermann's work he was gazing. Suddenly his face grew white, and he stumbled over to the taffrail, gasping for breath. Unconsciously Eckermann went on sketching. In a minute I went up to Tannemeyer and said: "You look ill. Do you suppose you have a fever?" He looked beyond me for an instant, and then with a visible effort he dragged his thoughts back to the present and said, "What?"

I repeated my question. "Are you not well?"

"O, yes, I'm all right; why?"

"O, nothing; you look somewhat pale, that is all."

I felt somewhat ridiculous. I had hoped that he would have told me about the scene I had witnessed; but no, he made no mention of it. Presently out came his pencil and paper and he began to sketch, so I moved away. Then on repassing, a moment or two afterwards, I saw on Tannemeyer's paper the very scene which Eckermann had sketched: the three fakirs juggling with their snakes. This time there was nothing wrong in Tannemeyer's drawing.

I ran to Eckermann. "A moment!" I exclaimed. "Please let me see the sketch you have just made, only for a moment." He looked at me in surprise, but he gave it to me. I ran back to Tannemeyer and begged him for his sketch, and he gave it to me. Then, tremblingly, I compared them; they were marvellously alike; no one could say that both were not the work of the same hand.

I turned and showed them to Tannemeyer, and he—fainted.

I saw him falling, and as I sprang up to catch him I dropped the sketches. With the help of a comrade I got Tannemeyer down to the doctor's room and there I left him. I hurried back to find the sketches, but one of them—Tannemeyer's—was lost. Some of the sailors were looking at the other. I claimed it and brought it back to Eckermann, and told him the whole circumstance.

He listened in silence, and when I had finished he said: "How long will it be before we reach Colombo, do you suppose?" I looked at him in wonder. "I don't know," I said; "but why? What makes you ask such an irrelevant question after what I have just told you?"

"Well, what shall I say, then? Shall we talk about the weather?"

I was rebuked again. "Forgive me," I said, "some time I may learn to mind my own business."

"O, don't mention it," he returned, and then seeing that he was pale and nervous, I left him.

Returning that way shortly after, I saw him gazing abstractedly at his sketch.

Next day we heard that Tannemeyer was ill of a fever and was quartered in the ship's hospital.

And the ship sailed on.

Whenever I tried to talk to Eckermann after that he seemed absent-minded and uninterested, so it came to pass that our friendship waned.

Occasionally I asked for news of Tannemeyer, and heard that he was improving in health.

We had reached Colombo at last, and had stopped again for coal. As I stood at the taffrail watching the strange scenery a familiar voice greeted me, and there at my elbow was Tannemeyer.

"*Grüss Gott!* Tannemeyer," I cried. "Are you better? I rejoice to see you on deck." Yes, he was quite well again and glad to be out of the hospital.

As we stood there talking a crowd of natives came swimming up, and crying as they swam: "*À la mer! À la mer!*" Then a throng of soldiers and sailors ran over to where we were standing and began to throw pennies into the water, whereupon these natives would dive after them and fetch them between rows of gleaming teeth.

Tannemeyer had his hand on the taffrail, and in the crowd another hand had been laid upon it. As though this other hand had been a coal of fire Tannemeyer whipped his hand away and stood trembling. Yes, it was Eckermann who had touched him quite inadvertently.

Tannemeyer went back to the hospital and remained there for the rest of the voyage. Even at Saigon, where we sojourned for several days, he did not appear, so I began to forget both him and Eckermann.

Thus far our passage had been calm and pleasant; no storms, and even the heat had not been as great as we expected. But now, on entering the China Sea, rough weather began, so we remained much of the time below decks. As we coasted up along Annam we were able to see land nearly all of the way. I think we stopped at Hue, but I can remember nothing of it, not having been able to go ashore.

Soon we reached Haï-Phong, where we disembarked from the big "Colombo" and boarded a small river steamer. Here I saw Eckermann and Tannemeyer again. I noticed that they still held aloof from each other, but my interest in my new surroundings was so great that I thought of little else. I was taken up with trying to learn a vocabulary of Annamite words and phrases so as better to understand what I saw and heard.

Eventually, through artificial canals and natural streams we entered the Red River, or the *Song-Koï,* as it is called, and came rapidly up to Ha-Noï, where many of us were to remain. I expected Tannemeyer would have to stop there; but no, although he belonged to another regiment in Algeria, and would naturally be sent to a different district here, still by some most curious oversight, or strange fatality, he was still with us. At Son-Tay, then, perhaps he would be changed; but not so, he was with us for good, it seemed. Well, I was glad, for I thought that if he and Eckermann remained together, some explanation of their actions toward each other might result. But seldom now did my mind dwell on anything but the unfamiliar beauty of the country and the incomprehensible chatter of the natives, many of whom were with us on the boat acting as engineers, cooks, pilots, etc.

Chinamen, too, were there as clerks and officers. These wore very wonderful garments. Somehow I had got away from the commonplace things of life, and, yes, there were stranger things in the world than the little mystery I had been studying.

It was in the dry season of the year, and when we had reached

Ba-Cat-Hat,—or Vie-Trie, as it is now called,—just where the Lo-Ciang empties into the Song-Koi, we could go no farther by boat; already we had been stuck fast in the bed of the river more than once. So to Hong-Hoa we must go afoot, and there we would be directed to the various posts we were to occupy. Ah, after nine long weeks of sea voyage we were joyful to be able to march, in such weather, through such a country.

Well, whom should I go with? Luick and Roebke had gone off together, and Siegfried was starting with Haas. While I stood hesitating, Tannemeyer came along and proposed that he and I should march together, help each other over streams and bogs, etc. I had a misgiving at first; I would rather have gone with Eckermann.

I always felt there was something uncanny about Tannemeyer ever since he had made the sketch.

Eckermann was a strong, handsome fellow, with a quick perception, so that he could always grasp my meaning before I spoke it,—nay, better than I could speak it, for my tongue often blundered over German genders. Tannemeyer was slower of comprehension, I thought, and his conversation was not easy to follow; this was owing to a peculiar accent and to a way he had of letting the final word or syllable die on his tongue unuttered. He had a well-featured face, but a look of great sadness gleamed in his dark, melancholy eyes.

I was somewhat surprised when he proposed to march with me, for since his second illness I had seldom spoken with him. I am afraid I did not express much pleasure in my voice nor in my glance when I acceded to his proposal, for he noticed it and made as if to draw back; but with as much sugar on my tongue as I could collect I begged him to march with me, saying we would go famously together; and so we did.

Never can I forget the charm of his companionship on that march. His mind opened and expanded under the influence of our surroundings, and it revealed to me delicacies and beauties I had never known. Wherever had he learned this subtle tact, this forgetfulness of self, this exquisite manner? He had mystified me on the ship, but now he dazzled me. He knew my moods by intuition,—when to be silent and when to speak; what to say and what to keep from saying. I *saw* the wonders of the landscape, but he put them into words for me so that I not only saw, but *felt*.

There were strange birds singing in the thickets, wild new tunes I had never heard before; and then Tannemeyer would sing an echo of their music till my heart leaped and thrilled to hear him.

What! I asked. Was this a German? Surely not; only one of the Latin race could disclose so complex a character. I asked him about it; was he indeed a Bavarian? a *Baier?* Yes, for three generations his people had lived in Munich. But before that? He did not know—he had never thought to ask. Why? "Because I am trying to find a key to your character," I said. He looked at me in a surprised manner, wondering perhaps what was unusual in his character that it needed a key.

But already the walls of Hong-Hoa were in sight, and the enthusiasm of his manner abated perceptibly.

Once more he was the Tannemeyer of the ship. But the beauty of the country through which we had come and the fascination of his companionship had made an impression on my mind which years could not efface.

At Hong-Hoa we remained several days exchanging our Algerian uniforms for those of Tonquin.

Here I met some old comrades from Saïda, so the time passed quickly with new experiences each day. Would we go and drink *tschum-tschum?* Would we smoke opium,—or the Annamite pipe? Would we ride in a *pousse-pousse,* and take tea in an Annamite kitchen? Oh, there were countless things we might do. But the days passed, and we who had just arrived must proceed farther up the river. As far as Cam-Khé we went, and there we had to separate, some going to one post, and some to another. Most of us were for the same company, and we would probably meet again; nay, as we were all of us to be along the river, we would probably meet again, so no one thought much of the separation. About half of our number were to remain in the vicinity of Cam-Khé and the rest of us started on, Eckermann and Tannemeyer still with us. But Tannemeyer, it seemed, was to cross the river directly. He with a dozen others was to reënforce the post of Than-Ba.

We came to the junk which was to ferry them over; already some were aboard, and Tannemeyer was waiting for his turn. Then suddenly he dropped his rifle, gave a wild, hoarse cry, and came running back. Eckermann saw him coming towards him, stumbling as he ran, and he understood. His lips parted too as if to cry out, and in an instant they were sobbing on each other's necks. Such a passion of love, despair, and anguish, please God, may I never see; two strong men between whom never a word of friendship or affection had passed were now delirious with grief at the thought of separation. It was more than I could bear to see: I turned away to hide my own tears. It was soon over. Before the surprise caused by this scene was passed, Tannemeyer was in the junk and off from shore.

There was the suspicion of a laugh in the air, and the certainty of curious comment, and questions from the comrades; so before anything of this sort could happen I ran up to Eckermann and began to talk to him soothingly of indifferent things, giving him no time to answer me, and leaving no chance for the others to break in with questions; nay, most of them had tact enough to look aside and see nothing; but I gabbled on, flying from one subject to another, till Eckermann had recovered his mind from the ordeal it had just been through. He understood my motive, and thanked me with his eyes. By my presence of mind I had saved him from questions and ridicule, and he was grateful. Of course if I could have done it in some other way, and left him alone with his emotion, it would have been better.

All this time I was burning to question him myself, but by an effort I refrained, hoping he would confide in me. Once he stopped and looked me in the eyes. I was sure he was about to speak.

As well as I could I expressed sympathy and understanding in a glance, but he sighed deeply and went on.

I had been weighed in the balance and found wanting. He could not tell me what was on his mind, so I did not vex him by asking. During the rest of the way to Yen-Luong, where I was to remain, he and I marched together. He chose it so. I enjoyed his company in a measure, and would have enjoyed it more had he not been so absent-minded; hitherto he had been quick and alert of thought, but now while speaking his mind would wander and he would forget what he had started to say. I knew very well that all his thoughts were of Tannemeyer, but by no sign did I show that I knew it, nor did I mention Tannemeyer to him.

I have since regretted this, and I wish I had been less delicate in the matter, even at the risk of giving offence. Since light might have resulted; something might have prevented the outcome of the affair which was stranger than all that had gone before.

We reached Yen-Luong at last, and there I parted with Ecker-mann; he went on to Yen-Bay, the next port, where he was to be quartered. . . .

For a month or longer I remained at Yen-Luong before any-thing happened. Some of us fell sick with the fever, but I had no time for that; I was too busy studying the ways of the country.

Then it was reported that the Governor-General, M. de Lanes-san, was making a tour of the posts. Already he was at Cam-Khé and would soon arrive at Yen-Luong. It made a stir in the air when this news was told, but the excitement did not touch me,—no, a French dignitary might be seen in any place at any time; but a genuine Annamite dignitary, with his umbrellas and his palan-quin,—a *ton-doc,* for example,—would be something worth see-ing. Well, but M. de Lanessan would have Annamite personages in his suite, it was said. O, in that case I was open to enthusiasm.

So he arrived, this governor-general, and he complimented us on the order and cleanliness of our post; and then—God bless his kind heart!—he commanded extra wine and tafia for us.

A frowzy-headed little man as I recall him, with a pleasant manner of speech. We had been instructed in the manner of salut-ing him, with his proper title, and so on, and we were warned that all deference was his due. But military men have a way of regarding all civilians, even the highest, in a condescending, half-contemptuous way; and taking the cue from our officers we were no way overwhelmed by his presence among us. Had he been a military general now, we would have given him a different recep-tion. The French soldiery of Tonquin is piqued and jealous that there should not be a military government there, as in Algeria;

consequently there is a lack of unity and sympathy in the land. I saw, it is true, only a shadow of this; but there must be a substance in order to cast a shadow.

Before this governor-general left us, we heard rumors of a band of pirates having been seen farther up the river; so our captain deemed it wise to send some of us with him for an extra escort in case of an attack.

I was elated over this, for I should thus see some of the comrades at the other posts.

At Yen-Bay my first question was for Eckermann. Even as I spoke his name I saw him running toward me. All his bearing was joyful; indeed, he was radiant, not alone in his white uniform, but in his face and manner. Ah, this new life, so strange and enchanting, who would not be pleased by it? What, sickness? fever? O, no indeed; not he,—and in a week or so there would be pirate-hunting, with tigers thrown in! What more charming life could any one desire? True, there was a sad side to it. So many good comrades dying and being killed; but death had to come some time, so better die here than in one's bed at home.

"Have you heard anything from the others?" I asked.

"Only that Haas was drowned, and that Pillerel has been killed by sunstroke."

"Have you never heard any word from Tannemeyer?" I asked.

"No; what of him? quick!" and all Eckermann's manner changed, his face turned pale.

"O, nothing; I know of nothing," I answered, indifferently. "I guess he's all right. Drosz was up from Than-Ba last week, and he reported all well; we would have heard if it were otherwise. But say, has Tannemeyer never written to you?"

"No."

"Nor you to him?"

"No."

Then Eckermann grew sombre, and I spoke of something else.

Next day we continued our journey, the governor and his party in a *chaloupe*, and we following in Chinese junks. The scenery as we ascended became wilder and more picturesque, and I longed to have Tannemeyer with me that he might interpret it. What glowing thoughts it would have brought to his mind! With what gorgeous sentences he would have described it! And I—I was not quite blind to it, only it oppressed me, and I wearied of it, and desired to return to commonplace sights.

We went as far as Traï-Hut and then returned. As we halted at Yen-Bay on our way back, I resolved to have an understanding with Eckermann. Yes, I would beg him to give me a kind message for Tannemeyer, whom I should probably see on my way down the river. I went up to the casern and called out: "Halloo! Eckermann, where are you?" I was in a hurry, for we had only an hour to stay. "Eckermann!" I cried. "Where's Eckermann?" I looked at the comrades who stood stupidly staring at me. "Where is he?" I demanded. "Can't one of you tell me where he is?" I read fear and consternation in their faces. Then one who had yellow hair and a soft voice came to me and whispered: "Are you Eckermann's friend?"

"Yes, yes; for God's sake tell me what you mean. Is he—is Eckermann ill?"

"No; not now, he shot himself yesterday through the heart—we buried him this morning." . . .

And now what should I say to Tannemeyer? And how should I tell him this awful thing?

Vainly I had sought in Yen-Bay for some clew to Eckermann's suicide; no one could throw the least light upon it. There had been no letters for a week; he could have heard no bad news. They said, forsooth, it was insanity, yet could not tell of any change in his manner.

I was sick with grief and horror, and now here we were at Than-Ba, and what should I—what could I say to Tannemeyer? I hoped he would have heard the news already, and that my lips need not tell him. I asked cautiously whether any word had been heard from up river. No, nothing for weeks; and then I ran up to the pagoda where the soldiers were posted.

I found Tannemeyer sketching in a corner.

He sprang up as he saw me and ran and embraced me in true German fashion.

"How goes it?" I repeated.

"O, very good, I think. I have an Annamite grammar, and I will soon know something of the language, and then the scenery! O, yes, I am quite happy; we have a good officer, and there is always something new to interest me. You have been up the river, you say, as far as Traï-Hut? I wish I had been with you. Did you—did you stop at Yen-Bay?"

"O, yes; and I too wish you had been with me. I wished it continually. You would have helped me to understand what it meant, you would have revealed the secret of all that beauty. Ah, what you see here is nothing to what I have seen; you must go farther north.

"'That's the appropriate country; there man's thought,
  Rarer, intenser,
Self-gathered for an outbreak, as it ought,
  Chafes in the censer.'

"But you don't know English. (My God! how should I tell him!) That's from one of our greatest poets; do you know him? Robert Browning? But I dare say he has not been translated into German. Why, there are even English people who have not read him. But, then, not all of you in Germany read from Jean Paul, do you?" I stopped, out of breath.

"Did you say you had halted at Yen-Bay?" he reiterated.

"O, yes, it's a very fine post, Yen-Bay; quite the best on the river. They have not to live in bamboo *canias* as we do at Yen-Luong; they have two large caserns there, built of brick, quite as good as any in Algeria. By the way, have you heard any news from Saïda?"

"Did you see Eckermann at Yen-Bay?" And so it had to come. Nay, in spite of my fencing he had read it already in my eyes. I crept up close to him and put my arm on his shoulder, and I told him all the fearful tidings. I thought he was going to fall, and I pressed closer to him and took his hand. He was not conscious any longer of my presence; he looked beyond me, off into space—far off into eternity he gazed. Then slowly he stood up and went outside. I watched him as he leaned over the parapet and stared down at the river. I had seen grief often and often, and, pity me! I had seemed to feel it; but never anything like this, never anything so awful as Tannemeyer's grief as he stood gazing on the river—the very air was full of it. I sat within the doorway, shuddering. No, no; it could not last, and there, while I looked at him, Tannemeyer turned and waved me farewell. A pistol was in his right hand. I saw a flash and heard a report; the next instant Tannemeyer lay dead in my arms.

THE COOLY

One morning it was made known to the captain that three coolies from the water-carriers were lacking. Thereupon he sent some of us down to the *lie-thung* (mayor?) of the village to bid him send us three other coolies. As we entered the *lie-thung's* house he was just fastening up his hair, in a Grecian knot you would have said.

He smiled a nervous welcome as he stopped in his toilet, and motioned us to be seated on the broad platform, on which his bedclothes were still lying. When he had served us tea from a porcelain pot, we told him, in "pigeon" French, what we wanted.

What! three more coolies? O, impossible; there was not one to be had in all the village. Of the three who were missing, one had been drowned the night before in the river, another had broken his arm, and the third had the fever. . . . Alas, no; there were no more coolies in the village. But in the neighboring villages? we suggested. Ah, there he had no jurisdiction; he was only the poor *lie-thung* of Yen Luong, and our captain's most obedient servant—*fai, ni?*

O, exactly; quite so, we assured him; and then we let him know our captain's full order; namely, that if he failed to send us three coolies, he himself should be taken and forced to do the work of three.

Oo-tia Buddha! Was this possible? Would we force him, the chief magistrate of his village, to labor with his hands—to do coolies' work? Had we neither pity nor justice? no bowels at all? no hearts?

And think, now! How in the name of Buddha could he help it, if the lazy coolies must fall into the river—and take the fever? Was he to—O, no, it could not be possible; we had only made a French joke—ha, ha! Never could the kind captain think—ah—

And there he stopped his whimpering, for he saw in our faces that it was French earnest, and no joke at all.

So he said if we would come with him he would see; yes, he would try what was to be done. Then we went out with him into the village.

First we found the cooly who had the fever; he was lying in the sunshine, shivering pitifully, quite unable to stand up. The *lie-thung* talked at him for a long time in tones of indignation and displeasure; all of which drew nothing but groans from the poor wretch. Finally the *lie-thung* gave him a kick, and turned to us with a smile. He had an idea.

"Come," he said, and led us to the house of the village school-master. I forget the Annamite name for him.

Why, of course the school-teacher could carry water for us well enough, anyway till the fever left the cooly. Certainly it would be more in keeping for a poor school-teacher to turn cooly than for a *lie-thung!*

That was his idea.

But we found this school-teacher to be an old, a very old man; far too feeble for our use.

"Him one good cooly, *nieh?*" whispered this miserable *lie-thung*.

The old man looked at us in wonder, while his long, fleshless fingers rattled the beads of an abacus.

As we stood there considering what we had better do, the schoolmaster's son came in. He was a bright-faced fellow of sixteen years, perhaps, strong of limb and quick of movement.

"Him one better good cooly; take him *nieh?*" insinuated this abject *lie-thung*.

Yes, we said, we would take him; but when our intention was made known the father fell at our feet and implored us to spare his son; saying that he and his family were not of the cooly class; saying that they worked not with their hands; that the shame of such work would kill them; saying, also, that his son was but a child,—his little one, his *tin-yow*,—never able to do this work of carrying water. Surely we would have pity. Pity? Yes, I suppose we felt it, but, alas! we had no permission to show it. Turnkeys and soldiers and hangmen must all shrug their shoulders and disclaim responsibility; and if their hearts ache over it, they, in turn, are to be pitied.

Seeing no relenting in our faces, the father said he would go in his son's stead. We laughed at this, explaining that the lad was the stronger, and so more suitable for our purpose. Up to this time the son had been passive; but we could see the blood come and go in his face, and the light in his eyes gleamed and faded while we talked. Then, as his father's proposal to go in his place became clear to him, he started forward, gathered his father up from our feet and stood between him and us.

"Me good cooly, come!" he said.

Then we went out together, leaving the old man to lament.

Well, here was one cooly, but we must still have two others, and we advised the *lie-thung* to make haste and find them, else—

We were passing through the marketplace, and there he laid hold of a battered old *kongoï,* saying she would do for a cooly, that already she had worked as one. She was a vision of dirt and rags, and her face—*ouf!* She said she was able and willing to go, if she could be sure of getting the right number of *sapiques* for her work.

Therefore we did not let her sex stand in the way of it, and straightway we engaged her.

Then, as we stood wondering where we would find the third cooly, and half inclined to force the *lie-thung* to the task, a poor rice-planter came along. He had been buying a pair of paper shoes, all ornamented with gold and silver tinsel, which he intended, I dare say, as an offering to Buddha; he seemed in a great hurry to go home and present them. That misfortune should meet him on his pious errand was very sad; but Buddha gets so many paper shoes offered to him, that one pair more or less can never matter. So we reasoned, and so reasoned the *lie-thung,* for he whispered: "Him three good coolies—*nieh!*"

So we persuaded the farmer to change his plan and come with us.

Here, then, were our three coolies: a farmer, an old woman, and a young boy. The *lie-thung,* chuckling over his own escape, bade us a hasty good-morning, and returned to his tea and his toilet. We went up to the post with our coolies. . . .

The name of the schoolmaster's son was Mot-li, but for no obvious reason we called him Charlot. He proved nearly equal to the task imposed on him. It was indeed sad to see how his veins stood out and his muscles were strained as he struggled up the hill with the heavy buckets.

Our post was on a high bluff, and all the water needed had to be brought up from the Red River (the Song Koï) which ran below. Twelve coolies were kept at this work from early till late. There was an overseer—a *caï-cooly*— to spur them on with a rattan should they flag in the toil. I saw Charlot on the evening of that first day; there were dark purple welts on his back where the rattan had stung him; and his shoulders, where the bamboo pole had rested, were all swollen and bloody. Not having been trained to such work, it was doubly hard for him.

Yet he came back the next day, and his father went to plead with the *lie-thung* for his release. The *lie-thung* referred the matter to the captain, but finally took the bribe and promised to find some one to replace Mot-li.

But on that second day of water-carrying, as Charlot was swaying up the hill with his load, the captain came riding down and saw him. He was gracious enough to say that such work was not suitable for one so young, and that Charlot might be employed as *boy-quat*. This meant that he could pull the *punkah*, or great fan, in the officers' dining-room; and when not working at that, he could act as scullion in the captain's kitchen.

This change was made; and as Charlot was able to speak a little French, and was, moreover, of a pleasing countenance, it was probable that he would obtain preferment. From a cooly he might mount to an interpreter—or even to a *caï-cooly*. Anyway, he seemed contented, and was exact and careful in his new work.

The *kongoï* and the rice-planter were soon released from their engagement, but Charlot remained with us. We all encouraged him, and showed him favor; so he came to be glad that the change had been made in his life. Then, as hope and happiness had returned to him, and as everything seemed to go well, it all came to a sudden end. One afternoon, at the flood-time of the year, Charlot stood watching how the great current below went sweeping past.

There were great trees, pieces of junks, carcasses of dead animals, all sorts of fragments, with now and then a human form, all floating past on the surface of the river. As he stood there watching the awful panorama, the chief cook of the captain's kitchen came out and disturbed his musing.

"How many, Charlot?" he asked.

"*Nam,*—five, me see five! last one, him cooly! *Oo-tia!*" answered Charlot, who had been counting the floating corpses.

Then the cook sent him down into the bamboo grove to gather dry sticks with which to make a fire in the morning.

Away went Charlot, singing as he went some monotonous wail which passes in Tonquin for music.

While with us he had learned to sing "*La Marseillaise*" (after a fashion of his own), but this afternoon he was gloomy; he had been looking at death and was afraid; so he sang a song of his own people, doleful to hear.

As the cook stood in the doorway of his kitchen he listened; vaguely and more indistinctly the notes came up as Charlot descended.

And then, suddenly, instead of the final refrain which the cook waited for, he heard a loud, prolonged shriek which chilled the blood in his veins, albeit the hot fire was at his back.

He looked down into the plain, and, after a moment of intense expectation, he saw a fearful thing: a great tiger came bounding out of the grove, and ran across the dry rice-field to the forest beyond. Charlot was clutched in his mouth and his head was hanging lifeless. . . .

And the next morning there was a sorrowful sound heard without the post,—the sound of an old man's bitter grief.

There in the dust, without the gate, sat the old schoolmaster asking for his son,—his little one,—his *tin-yow!*

And there he sat all day long, and for many following days, crying to every one who went by for Mot-li,—for Mot-li!

Then one day this wailing was not heard, for the schoolmaster lay dead—there by the outer gate of the palisade.

"LE BUIF"

"Ne sutor ultra crepidam."

We had been to Ka-Dinh. I must shrink even now when I remember Ka-Dinh, and all we had to endure in going there. As usual, I had quarrelled with O'Rafferty. Geniets had remained at Yen-Bay, Siegfried also; thus there was no one in our squad with whom I cared to talk. I must march in silence, then, listening to others, and learning my world. Behind me came Rotgé, a burned-out Parisian, and after him marched poor Richet, of whom I tell what follows.

A dull, silent fellow, too stupid to resent Rotgé's gibings. When we were in garrison at Yen-Luong, he was cobbler *"en pied"* for the company. This was why Rotgé never called him anything but *le buif.* His shoulders were bent, and as he trudged along his bearing was no way martial. He did not appeal to me strongly, hardly at all, indeed, and so I never tried to turn the tide of Rotgé's sarcasm. Richet would smile at it in a mild way, dimly seeing that he was being lampooned, but more flattered than offended thereat.

"O, but you are a hard-head, Rotgé, and I know you—hey?"

Then Rotgé would glance at me, but I had not heard.

At length we reached Yen-Bay, and there we were confounded to learn that Richet had been named corporal in our absence. What! surely not Richet *le buif!*

"Yes, truly, who else?"

Had we been told that Boulanger had been renominated minister of war we had not wondered; but this! Why, we had not even known that Richet's name was on the list of the *élèves caporaux.* All the same, so it was, and we could only wonder what the result would be. The result was sad. Little souls are sooner caught by ambition than great ones, just as a straw hut will take fire more readily than a stone palace.

At Yen-Luong we had all found Richet so stupid, that unless we had a pair of *brodequins* to be mended we hardly ever spoke to him. He talked in a slow, drawling voice, not pleasant to hear.

He was generally alone, yet when he had earned a little money by supplementary cobbling he would spend it freely with Rotgé, or with any one, and at these times companions never failed him. But he was not morose at other times, only dull and silent. Well, well; and now he was no longer Richet *le buif,* but Corporal Richet, if you please! We shrugged our shoulders and sniggered. He himself was as much astonished as we, but instead of finding some means whereby to reject his nomination, he took it in perfect serious-ness, for forthwith he began to believe in his own ability, and, yes, he would demonstrate to us that he was less stupid than we supposed—*hein?* Then on several occasions the other corporals proved to him that he was unwise in trying to carry it through; they made it quite plain to him that he was an *imbécile,* so he spoke at times of renouncing his rank and going back to his cob-bling—h'm. . . . If he had done so, all might have gone well; but he kept on. He was able to keep on with it because we were still on the march, so his service was simple enough; also, the others helped him. Then a day came when he was given the *ordinaire* in his charge; in other words, he must attend to the distribution of rations for his company. This is often the work of a sergeant, but every corporal should be able to do it, since all that is required for it is a little knowledge of "the three R's." But, ho! poor Richet was aghast. He knew the prices of sole-leather, but little else. He never could have performed this new service had the others withheld their help. On looking back, we saw how this charge must have weighed upon him mightily, far more than we imagined at the time. It was then that Sergeant Dreck began his thieving, began to steal from our rations, thinking that all the blame would fall on Corporal Richet. Wine he stole, and tafia, and canned meats, and who knows what all. Richet saw the deficit and trembled.

We, however, knew that he was quite innocent, and we all felt at once that Sergeant Dreck was the greedy one who had pilfered from our stores. Richet was deeply moved about it, and he spoke of paying us from his own poor pocket. We resented this, and tried to pass it over. Still he fretted about it, and his work weighed upon him more than ever.

During our long, wearisome marches Richet was often unwell,

but his silly ambition made him hold out, even when his physical forces were far from equal to the effort. Pounding leather on a lapstone had not trained him for marching, so he suffered more than the rest of us. But just before we came back to Yen-Bay for the last time, he said he would not return with us to Yen-Luong; he said he had a cold, and he would remain at Yen-Bay and enter the infirmary there.

We laughed at his assurance; we were all fit enough for the infirmary, but we knew that a cold or even a *bronchite* would not be a sufficient reason for getting in. But as Richet was so sure of his affair, we said nothing to daunt him. We were used to his moods by this time, and noticed nothing new. I remembered afterwards how excited he was that night,—all about two Corsicans of another squad who began to fight over a game of chess. We would have let them strangle each other in peace, but not so Richet; he jumped between them and cried out: "I forbid you! I am Corporal Richet, and I forbid you! I forbid you, I say!" So much energy and noise coming from the phlegmatic Richet surprised me, and astonished the Corsicans so much that they forgot their quarrel. The next day Richet was grieved and chagrined because he was not admitted to the infirmary. We pursed our lips and looked askance.

On leaving Yen-Bay we learned that Sergeant Dreck had been stealing our rations again; so we threw it in his teeth, and jeered at him openly. Richet looked gloomy and almost desperate; he still had charge of the *ordinaire,* and by this time he could manage it if not interfered with. But Dreck was unabashed, and said that our corporal was a fool. "So between a fool and a knave we may go hungry," we snarled. "And you are not the fool!" In settling back into garrison life we forgot all about Richet and his new rank.

There came a day which was very hot; a thick, stifling vapor seethed through the air; the sun seemed quite near to us, for through the vapor we could look straight at it and never blink. There it was, just overhead, a ball of pink fire spinning in space. The river below us ran quickly past, as if it feared to be turned into steam before it could reach the sea.

The rice-fields beyond had been under water the day before, but their moisture was now fast disappearing into the air. I put wet napkins on my head and crept away to a dark place. . . .

Next day I was all right, but many others were on the sick-list. One came in and said that Corporal Richet was drunk ever since the night before.

That seemed strange, for since the Chinaman had been evicted from his canteen down by the river, we had no means of getting drink; and, thinking it over, Richet had never been a drinking soldier. But there,—as we could hear him gabbling nonsense out at the kitchen, I concluded that he must indeed be drunk. How purblind we are! We see things happening day after day, yet when the natural effect of such happenings arrives, we gape at it as if we had seen no foreshadowing of it.

For half a day, then, we believed Corporal Richet to be drunk, when indeed he had become a jabbering, gibbering idiot.

At the first there was a grain of sense or consequence in his talk, but by evening he was mad as a hatter. And still he would say a thing which would make us laugh; we are ever so ready to laugh, that the grin on a skull may start us. But again he would begin to talk about his mother—and that was gruesome. The strange thing was that Richet should be talking at all, for never had he talked so loud before. Some of us had never heard him speak till then; but now how he raved! This is the way he went on: "I will beg you to remark one thing. I'm no fool—not I. I am cute, I tell you. Look here!—but no matter,—ha, ha! I can do anything—everything— and I'm not afraid—no—I'm a corporal, hey?—well, I'll become a sergeant too, and so on up the line. I'm not a fool, I tell you; I'm cute—I'm too sharp for you. I know the world,—and there's my mother. O, she'll be pleased with me now—for I'm going home, I tell you,—yes, I've got my discharge, and I'm going home—home to see my mother. How she'll laugh! She'll be satisfied with me now—she always said I was no fool, and she knows me. How she'll laugh! ha! ha! ha!"

He would begin these short phrases in a low voice, but as he went on he would increase the sound so that the last words were loud and triumphant. It was a woeful thing to hear, and when we could stand it no longer we persuaded poor Richet to go to bed in the adjutant's room, which was vacant.

"In the adjutant's room? Why not! for I'll soon be an adjutant too, ha, ha!"

Next day he was sent to Yen-Bay, but he soon returned on his way to the hospital at Ha-Noï. He was pale and sleepy and hollow-eyed—and still ceaselessly gibbering. And still I can hear him say: "How she'll laugh! ha! ha! ha!"

So, had he never gone beyond his last, it would have been better for him, and for his mother.

A DREAM

"And without a parable spake he not unto them."
—Matt. xiii. 34.

And so I lay down to sleep with my head pillowed in the hollow of Buddha's left foot,—there where he sat cross-legged on the ground.

A dim radiance flickered within the pagoda, partly from three rush-lights, and partly from our camp-fire without the walls. From where I lay I could see, indistinctly, the forms of seven other images, ranged on one side, and opposite them, and far in the back, were many more immortals which I could not see; but all of them, like Buddha, were wrapped away in Nirvannah, with never a consciousness of any intrusion, or of any desecration in their sanctuary.

Outside I could hear the irrelevancies of my comrades; they were telling each other what delectable things they would eat when they were back in Paris; and one recounted in a lingering voice the whole beautiful *menu* of a three-franc dinner at the *Palais Royal. Ouf!* I tried to shut my ears to all that, and I thought that I too would fain find Nirvannah; so I turned, saying I would sleep. But my eye caught sight of another group of images.

There was a central female figure, framed about with smaller shapes which represented the human passions; so I understood it. See! there was Gluttony, with Drunkenness reeling above him. Anger and Lechery and all the rest in a hideous circle, whence the Woman looked forth in sad serenity. What was it? Had she given birth to these? Or were they—

And so I slept.

And I dreamed that you and I were standing together on a wide, barren seashore. Far away from us the sea rolled peacefully in, making no sound; and very far away to the left we saw the misty outline of a cliff.

Suddenly I knew the place, and I was afraid. Gérôme has made a picture of it; only in the place where we were standing he has painted a lion,—a fierce lion, with out-sprawled legs and lashing tail. In my dream I shuddered lest it were behind us and I should see it. As we stood, the cliff seemed to advance towards us; nearer and nearer it came, and watching it I forgot the lion. Then, moved by a quick impulse, we ran forward to meet it. As we sped along, the wind arose and blew up clouds of red sand; but we did not stop.

I thought: "Ah, we are in Algeria, and this is a sirocco; there is nothing to fear." Then, through these sand-clouds, I saw that the cliff had changed into a great stone temple of strange construction. I looked at you in wonder and said: "See, it is not a mosque, nor a marabout; neither is it a pagoda, nor a synagogue; for whose worship or honor can it have been built?" I waited, but you made me no reply. I saw then that you did not hear me; you did not know you were there; you were asleep or entranced, without consciousness of anything; you did not even feel my grasp upon your arm. All the horror of the unknown came upon me, and clutching your hand I hurried you along.

Presently we came close to the temple; deeply cut in its granite walls I traced strange figures and hieroglyphs.

Before us was a wide courtyard, flanked by two wings of the temple; it was paved with large squares of red-veined marble, and in the centre stood the image of a cow carved from stone, short and thick of body and perched on legs, or rather on four sculptured columns which raised it up to the top of the temple. Then I turned again to you and said: "O, I know now what it is, and where we are; this is the Bull Apis, and this temple was built for its worship. You see we are in Egypt, in Ancient Egypt. Come, we will go into the temple." But lo! as I spoke you had gone, and the Bull Apis had gone, and I was alone.

Before me the cold granite walls still remained, but carved now with dragons and symbols of Buddha's worship. As I stepped upon the marble slabs of the courtyard, blood oozed out of them and clung to my feet. When I saw this I stood still, unable to move for fear. Then slowly the two great doors of the temple opened towards me, and a priest came out. On his head was a towering red turban, and I supposed him to be a Brahmin,—only how came he into Egypt?

As I looked in his face, all my fear vanished, for in his eyes I saw nothing but the purest, tenderest love. Infinite sympathy was in his glance, and I was fain to abase myself at his feet.

But I held back, I knew not how. Something, many things about him surpassed my comprehension. Senses and faculties were his whereof I had no knowledge. Ah! I thought, but if I go into the temple I shall learn them; I shall acquire them for myself; I shall be like him, and shall wear a towering red turban! He knew my wish before I could speak it, and motioned for me to enter.

The doors closed upon me, shutting him out. I found myself in an inner court, which was paved with porphyry. There were no windows, or any lamps; yet all the place was filled with purple light.

Here were more priests, all clothed like the first one, and lying on the floor in front of them were six Roman cardinals, all asleep, their hats hung on pegs in the wall above them. In an instant I understood; already I was acquiring new powers of perception. These cardinals were missionaries, who had come to convert the "heathen" priests of this temple. They had been preaching, all of them together, and were sleeping now after their ineffectual exertion.

As I stood looking at them, one at the end, warned in his sleep of my presence, awoke, and, raising himself on his elbow, he waved me back with a sweeping gesture. He and his companions, with their hats, seemed strangely out of place, yet I did not smile. Gently one of the priests made him lie down again, and re-covered him with the silk blanket which his gesture had displaced.

I asked this priest whether I must remove my shoes before penetrating further into the temple, for I saw piles and rows of shoes and sandals at the door.

"Yes," he said, "for they are stained with blood."

Then all at once I felt myself going, rushing down a long corridor, together with a mass of strange, unfamiliar people. I could hear them talking, but understood no word. But it seemed that I should soon come to know everything; once let me reach the inner sanctuary, where already I could see moving forms, and then all tongues and all mysteries would be plain to me.

Suddenly I stopped and let the people sweep past. I felt the cold pavement under my bare feet. I wanted to remember where I had left my shoes. I was sure I had removed them, for there were blood-stains on my hands; but where were they? I could not think. So I was drawn in opposite directions; the intense desire to learn what was beyond drew me forward. I could even see through a glass wall portions of a strange ceremony. A man clothed in cloth of gold stood before something and worshipped. Confusedly I could hear what he was saying. One word, always the same, he kept repeating in a solemn chant. I strained hard to hear it. Buddha? Brahma? Jehovah? Jove? Allah? No, neither of these; and yet all of these, and many others, all expressed in this same word. Ah, this word, if I could learn it, would be the key of all things known and unknown. I took another step forward, and felt again the cold flagstones under my feet; and then the necessity of finding my shoes forced me back. Well, I would return and find them, and still be in time to learn this word. Back I flew to the doors and began a hurried search among the rows and piles of dusty shoes. I would know mine by the blood on them, I thought; but I looked in vain.

Shoes and sandals of every shape and size; but mine were not with them,—none of them were stained with blood. Wildly I ran from pile to pile, from row to row,—my search was useless.

Then the people began to come out, and I saw with dismay that the rite was over. It had ended while I stood turning over dusty shoes. This was remorseful. I stood back in a corner and wept, with my face to the wall. Then I thought: "I will wait here till every one is gone, and if any shoes be left, I will take them." Soon I heard the outer doors close, and looking around I saw my own shoes lying near by. Eagerly I seized them, and was hurrying away when one of the cardinals came and said they were his shoes. "No," I cried, "for mine have marks of blood on them, as you may see." He snatched them from me, but in an instant he let them fall and started forward and stopped. I looked to where his gaze was turned, and saw a row of mummies standing against a wall. As we both stared at them they fell forward on their faces and flew into fragments at our feet. The cardinal backed away, and I saw him changing into a painted mummy himself. As he recoiled he fell backwards over my shoes and flew into fragments just like the others. . . .

Then I awoke in a great trepidation. The camp-fire was burned out, but the rush-lights showed me that all was well. I could hear the deep breathing of my comrades, asleep near by, and the quiet tread of the sentinel as he passed to and fro outside.

Thoughtfully I turned and kissed my pillow, and slept in peace till morning.

DE PERIER

"If I can gain Heaven for a pice,
  Why need you be envious?"

I was sitting, one day, while journeying to Tonquin, on the ledge
of a two-storied hen-coop in the stern of the vessel. There were
other hen-coops on the opposite side, and sheep-pens farther
along; wisps of hay were sticking to the bars of the pens, and
paddy—that is, unthreshed rice—was scattered about the coops.
At Singapore we had taken more sheep aboard,—an Asiatic breed,
with broad, flat tails. Were the chickens "Brahmas," or "Cochin-
Chinas," or "Plymouth Rocks"? I could not tell. I saw that they
looked low-spirited as they crouched in a corner, and I called,
"Biddy! biddy!" and "Chick! chick!" but they gave no heed.

Soldiers of the Foreign Legion and of the Marine Infantry
went strolling up and down the deck, while others squatted in
groups playing *loto* or *piquet.* Presently a fellow dressed as a *chasseur d'Afrique* came and perched on the hen-coop opposite and
began to stare at me. I liked his face, so I stared back at him. I had
noticed him frequently before, particularly as he was the only one
of his corps on board, and I had intended to ask some one about
him, but had forgotten. Now, as we sat there, dangling our feet
listlessly, we took each other's measure. What his judgment was
he told me afterwards; what mine was I kept to myself till now. I
thought his face was unusually handsome, having only two defects:
a sensual mouth and a weak chin. I had seated myself up there
with the hens for the purpose of reading "Minna von Barnhelm,"
but when this *chasseur* came along, I stuck the book between the
bars of the coop, and stared uninterruptedly till O'Rafferty passed,
and I called his attention with the tip of my toe and asked him
who my *vis-à-vis* was, and *"que diable sient il faire dans galère."* I
knew O'Rafferty would soften to a bit of French, so for the sake
of the quotation I humored him.

"O, he? I don't know exactly. Why do you ask me? Did you
think I knew him?"

"No," I answered. "I did not suppose you would know him, or would care to tell if you did. I only asked you because I was too lazy to get down and ask some one else."

Then O'Rafferty went on, and my right toe tingled. The chickens came forward, and picked at "Minna," so I rescued my book and began to read.

But pshaw! with that fellow's big gray eyes gazing at me I could not read, and I did not care to look at him any longer. So I got down and went forward. I found Gregoire, a big Belgian of my company, sitting in a shady corner, reading an ancient copy of "Le Figaro." I squatted down beside him, and asked him what was the news.

"O, nothing new," he yawned; "the Pope is still in Rome, it seems, and Bismarck at Berlin."

"Delighted to hear it; but say, who is the *chasseur* with the white hands and the big eyes? But as there is only one, I need not describe him. Do you know anything about him?"

"Yes; shall I introduce you? I know him well enough; he's a splendid chap; he killed an Arab—a *spahi;* that's why he's here. His colonel got him off that way. He's to go to Ha-Noï and enter the marine infantry there. He's a journalist, I think. Shall I introduce him?"

"Perhaps," I said, "but not now. I want to take in what you have told me. How did he come to kill the *spahi?*"

"O, I don't know the details; it seems the *spahi* was jealous, and thought De Perier—that's his name—was flirting with his wife, or trying to; so he called De Perier a *sale roumi,* and De Perier slapped him, so they had to fight, and De Perier spitted him clean through. Then there was a fuss. Caïd somebody or other of the tribe of I don't know what, wanted vengeance. But the colonel of De Perier's regiment was a friend of De Perier's papa, and so all the punishment he got was thirty days *au clan,* and then they shipped him off here to Tonquin, as you see, and he'll change his corps, that's all."

"Thanks, Gregoire," I said. "I'll tell you to-morrow whether I wish to be introduced to your friend or not."

"What's that? My friend? I did not say he was my friend, did I? I know him somewhat, but there is no friendship between us."

"O, I beg your pardon, but as you praised him so much, I supposed you felt kindly towards him."

"And so I do feel kindly towards him; but that is far from having him for my friend."

Well, I noticed as we sailed that every one felt kindly towards De Perier, yet no one seemed to make a friend of him; at least he was generally alone. Of course, being of a different corps, there was some reason for this; and yet one would expect that, being in the same squad (or *plat,* as we say at sea) with a few of the marine soldiers, some of them would have fraternized with him; but not at all; they left him quite alone.

When it came to the point of having Gregoire introduce me or not, I refused. No; De Perier attracted me in a way, but he repelled me at the same time.

"No, Gregoire," I said; "there is something queer about him. I don't know what. You feel it yourself, and you don't know what it is. Well, I don't want to know."

After that I thought no more about De Perier till he was leaving us, at Ha-Noï. Then, as I watched the others disembarking, I saw him running about shaking hands with everybody, and with me too before I knew it, or had the presence of mind to dodge him.

"*Au revoir,*" he said; "I'll see you again."

"The deuce you will!" was what I thought, but I said: "Well, *au revoir.*"

I certainly never expected to see him again, and as nearly as I can remember I never wanted to. He was no more to me than a face in a crowd; a handsome face, perhaps, but not recalled with any delight. Yet we did meet again, as he predicted, and this was the way of it: I was sent to Ha-Noï to give testimony in a court-martial case, and as the trial was delayed for two or three months my stay there was prolonged.

I was quartered in the citadel with a company of marine infantry, and I had nothing to do but amuse myself and ward off mosquitoes.

One evening a tall "*marsouin*" came into our chamber and made himself free of a place on my bed, and forthwith he began to talk to me. I looked at him sharply, and tried to remember where

I had seen him before; he saw my hesitation and said: "What? You forget? But I told you I would see you again. Don't you recall the *chasseur* on board the 'Colombo'?"

"Yes, vividly," I assented; "but you're not he; you're not De Perier?"

"O, yes I am, and quite at your service."

Sure enough; he had the same large gray eyes, only now I saw another light in them: the pupils seemed larger, and the expression was somehow different. Moreover, the large sensual mouth looked drawn, and fell at the corners more than formerly; yet, of course, it was De Perier: his voice was not changed, and as he talked I recalled it.

"Say," he said, "why did you not let Gregoire introduce me to you on shipboard?"

I was taken aback by this sudden question.

"Did he tell you that I refused then?"

"No, he never spoke of you to me; but I knew what was in your mind. Don't you remember the day we sat staring at each other from opposite hen-coops? I came near saving you the trouble of asking O'Rafferty about me by coming over and telling you myself what I saw you wanted to know."

"But—but—but how did you know I asked O'Rafferty? Did he tell you?"

"Why, no; can't you understand? I read it all in your face."

"Indeed? You seem to have remarkably clear eyesight." And suddenly I turned and stared at him again straight in the eyes. "What," I asked, "do you read in my face now?"

"Why, you are wondering how it is that I have changed so: whether it is the climate; and whether I have the fever, and so on. Am I not right?"

"Quite right," I replied; "but you need not answer these questions till I ask them audibly."

I was vexed with him, and with myself, more than there was any reason for being; he saw it and said: "Come, let us go out for a walk; you do not wish to go to bed yet." I did not want to go out with him in the least; but neither did I wish to sit there talking with him. I turned my face away that he might not see what I was thinking, and then I opened my lips to make some excuse; but what I really said was, "Yes, let us go for a walk." Out we went; I felt the same repugnance to him that I had spoken of to Gregoire, and now I partly understood it; it was because he had the power of reading my thoughts, and forestalled me with answers and comments before I spoke. But that was not all. I kept thinking of Doctor Fell, and wondering whether he guessed it; perhaps he did, for he worked hard to amuse me, and make me reconsider my verdict; and when he had talked for a time about Algeria I did reconsider it. He struck the right note when he began about that country, and I listened with open ears. "O, yes," I said, trying him; "but here in Tonquin we have this wonderful vegetation, and in Algeria it is all barren plains."

"Wonderful vegetation! look at it! green, green, green—eternally green! and I am sick of it, and I burn to get back to my barren plains. There one is free—one can breathe; ah! wait till you know Algeria as I do and you will agree with me."

"But I agree with you now," I said. "I, too, prefer Algeria to any other land."

"Only not to France?"

"A thousand times to France."

"Ah, but you see my mother is in France, and so I"—

After that first evening I felt no more repugnance towards De Perier, and the days were long till the evenings when he would come and sit on my bed and talk. Sometimes he was on guard duty and could not come, but six evenings out of seven we were together.

Once I asked him about his prospects: what would he do when his service was finished?

"O, I shall probably never get out of my track; I shall reënlist."

"Reënlist!" I screamed; "but you told me you hated the life. You don't propose to try for promotion, do you?"

"Not at all. Yes, I do hate it, but what else can I do?"

"You frighten me! What else can you do? Why, you might better do anything than become brutalized here in the army! I thought Gregoire told me you were a journalist?"

"So I am—or so I was once; but that's a dog's life too; and then—but don't let us talk about it."

"As you choose," I said; "but how about your mother? You said she was in France; will you not wish to return to see her?"

"I said, please do not let us talk about my future; but since you will have it, I'll tell you that—that I"—

Then he got up and went out, and I saw him no more till the next day, which was Sunday; then he came in the afternoon and invited me to go out in town and call on some of his friends. No way loath I went with him.

I wanted to lead our talk back to where it had so suddenly ended the night before, but he started off on another track; he began to tell me of a girl whom he once wanted to marry—on whose account he was here. "Why," I interrupted, "from what Gregoire told me, I thought it was for killing an Arab that you were obliged to come here."

"O, yes; but if I had not been in Algeria I could not have killed the *spahi,* and if it had not been for Catrine I would not have been in Algeria. What says your English proverb? 'For ze want of ze ridère ze cheval was los',' hein!"

"Ah, quite so, I understand. By the way, do you not speak English?"

For my sins I asked it! Forthwith he began to recall Ollendorf's English, and he floundered about for a time in impossible sentences.

"O, excellent, excellent!" I exclaimed; "I admire your memory; but to go back to Miss Catrine; how was it her fault that you went to Algeria?"

"O, the old story: she loved some one else—at least she married him—and I had the misfortune to wound him in a duel. I had confidently hoped that he would kill me, but he didn't, as you see, so I went off to Algeria. What great lengths we go when once started; just like the rest of creation, we have to submit to the law of inertia, we—but here we are at Robert's; come in."

We were in a by-street, lined with low-roofed, Annamite dwellings.

We entered a large room just off the street, and I was introduced to Robert and to his Annamite wife. He was a middle-aged man, employed as a town clerk, or something. It was interesting to see how she deified him, and pleasing to see how kind he was to her; but nothing else about either of them attracted me. After the usual speeches of courtesy had been made, I found that Robert spoke English quite readily, and he was glad of a chance to show off his ability. All at once he whispered to me, "Have you known De Perier for a long time?"

"No, but be careful; he understands a little English; he will hear you."

"No; he is talking to my wife, he does not notice. If you had known him well, I would have asked you to help him, but as you are only an acquaintance"—

"Even so, I am willing to help him if I can. How does he need help?"

He looked at me sharply. "Don't you know? don't you see?" he whispered.

"Not in the least; I see he has changed somehow: he is not like what he was before coming here—I remember him on the voyage—but"—

"O, if you don't know what it is, I cannot tell you. I am sorry I spoke; please forget it."

"Certainly, I shall not mention it, but I shall be curious all the same. I have often heard him speak of you as his friend, but permit me to say that you were not greatly pleased to see him when we came in. O, no doubt you were cordial enough with the lips, but the light in your eyes went out. I used to feel quite as you do towards him, but lately I have grown to like him."

"And so do I; I like him, too, but"—

"But what? Speak out, man! You talk of him as if he were a murderer. I know that he killed an Arab, but it was in a duel, and"—

"O, I say there, you are not very polite, you others, with your English." It was De Perier who spoke.

"You are right," I said; "but please excuse us, 'tis so long since we have had a chance to speak it."

Alas! I saw that though De Perier had not understood, he had guessed what we were talking about. I was vexed with him for having taken me there, and with Robert for having dragged me into a false position. I was eager to get away, and so, for that matter, was De Perier. Before long we stood up to take leave. Robert's little boy came in just then, and he jabbered a jumble of French and Annamite to us, which relieved the strain, and we were able to come away laughing.

Robert seemed sincere in asking us to call again, and in an aside to me he asked if I would come alone the next day. I said yes, I would; but I did not feel very sure about it. I had had enough of Robert. As soon as we were on the street De Perier cried: "What did he say? Did he tell you?"

"Did he tell me what? I will tell you, De Perier, that your friend Robert does not please me at all, and I wish we had never gone near him. He hinted things—or something—about you, I don't know what—and you have hinted yourself. Last night you— but please don't think I am asking you to tell me what is in the wind."

"Well, see here," he cried; "it is in the wind, as you say, and if you remain at Ha-Noï you will hear it from some quarter; so I may as well tell you myself: *I smoke opium.*"

"Indeed!" I exclaimed. "The mountain was in labor and brought forth a mouse! You and your friend Robert make much ado about nothing."

"Ah, but you don't understand: I am a slave to it; I cannot live without it; *and it is killing me.*"

Yes, I saw it now. I had been blind and stupid not to have seen it before. Why, only coming down the river I had seen a Chinaman dying from this habit; but, pshaw! it could not be.

"Do you say," I asked, "that you *know* it is killing you, and you will not stop it?"

"No, I do not say that: I say I know it is killing me and I *cannot* stop it,—to stop it would be death, too, so far I have gone."

"But how—when do you smoke?"

"Every night; when I leave you I go straight to the pipe."

"But do your officers not know it? Has no one warned you, or tried to save you?"

"Yes, it is becoming known; but no; nothing can be done for me. There is no immediate danger, however, unless I were to be deprived of it."

"Ah, but in your position as a soldier, how easy it would be to deprive you of it! Suppose for some breach of discipline you were put into prison for a few days or longer?"

"Well, I have considered that possibility, and in such a case I would be obliged to eat opium instead of smoking it."

"Yes, but how procure it in prison, even for eating?"

"O, I am always provided with a certain quantity for fear of being taken unawares, as you suggest; but I know there are thousands of circumstances in which I might be forced to forego it. You know, I suppose—at least you have read,—that the after effects of the sleep are as horrible as it is heavenly. Well, the chief horror for me is the fear of having no more opium to smoke. I imagine that I am dying for lack of it, as I may be some day, and the agony and terror of this feeling are unspeakable. But that is only one of the horrors—and, pshaw! the delights are greater than the horrors, so why should I forego them? Don't speak; I know all you may wish to say. I have said it all to myself, often and often. I know it is a terrible state to be in. At least rational people so consider it. But what is reason, anyway? Yet no; why should I seek to defend myself? You cannot judge fairly till you are as I am, and then you will judge as I do. Why is it that certain of us were born with such weak wills that we run headlong to destruction? Were we not created for this?"

"O, for God's sake, De Perier!" I cried, "do not talk such infernal nonsense! You fool yourself if you think it is your fate to destroy yourself. I cannot say that if you were to blow out your brains at once there might not be some merit and virtue in that; but to kill yourself slowly, mind and body, as you profess to do, strikes me as being the madness of a fool."

"It is worse than that," he cried. "I am almost rational now, and I see almost as you do; but in a few hours, when the desire to smoke returns, then it is the madness of a devil which fills me, and I am not myself; or I am myself at such times and not now. I do not know. I know that some experience one thing, and some another. My case is exceptional. I cannot hinder my fate. I can only submit."

"O, yes," I sneered; "that is the plea that every one makes; but it is false. Indeed you flatter yourself; your case is no different from thousands of others; you"—

"Hold on! you are wrong, there," he cried. "Each case, each individual, is different in countless ways from every other individual; the circumstances of no two lives are just alike, and if you knew the details of my life—say, do you believe in inherited tendencies? But why should I seek to defend myself? I wish rather to condemn myself, and to warn you and every one from following in my path."

"But listen an instant," I said. "Is your case utterly hopeless? Can nothing—absolutely nothing—be done? Do you not desire now—now when you say you are almost rational—to stop in your course, to get back your strength and manhood?"

"I understand what you ask, but that is all; I have no desire for anything much, except for peace—and opium. What you call strength and manhood, what are they, after all, that I should desire them? Strength and manhood, forsooth! What are they for but to experience joy and pleasure withal, hein? O, yes; 'sane pleasures' and 'modest joys'—*Et in Arcadia ego!*—*Fichtre!* Are they to be compared in any way with the delights of opium? Never!"

"Alas! then I may hold my peace," I said, for to talk with him was like groping for a door in a blank wall; and then I shuddered. I, in my safety, felt so scornful, so unforbearing towards him. I was safe because I felt no desire to imitate him; yet if it were otherwise, would that be wonderful or surprising?

"Listen, De Perier," I said, "and try to understand what I mean. It is impossible that I should feel otherwise than disgusted with you. The old revulsion which I felt on the ship has returned to me; I know now why I feel it. But now I have another feeling in my heart for you—no, it is not pity: you need not wince—it is sympathy. Thus, even while I feel how terribly depraved you are, I have no stone to throw at you; not one.

"To me your fault seems very great, but that does not make it so; my standards are never what you or any one shall be judged by.

I am something of a Pharisee, perhaps, because I *am* thankful not to be as you are, just as I would be thankful not to have a broken leg or softening of the brain; you see, there is no scorn of you in it. In my way I may have worse defects than this of yours, and—I have not yet left Tonquin. Who can tell that I may not become as you are? It is always possible. Realizing this, I cannot condemn you without condemning myself beforehand. Now, see here: if you think that my companionship is of any value to you, I ask you to make use of it when you will, and as you will; but if you are indifferent, or can forego my society without loss, I ask you for my sake to do so. I believe that if I were to see you often I would grow used to the idea of opium, and—who is ever sure of himself? No; unless there be something to be gained for you by coming to see me, I will ask you not to come any more. This looks to be unkind; yes, it looks quite as if I threw you off because you were not good enough for me; but you know it is not so; you know—you must know that I care more for you now than I ever did before; and this is what makes your presence dangerous for me; being fond of you, I may easily grow used to your habit, I may just wish to try it—just to see; you know how easy it is to start on a bad road." . . .

To all this and much more De Perier listened in silence. We had come back by way of the lake, and there we sat down on a big stone bench to talk the matter over. I did not think he would regret the loss of my company; he had his opium to console him for any temporary disquietude.

See there! was I not half envious of him, of his ability to escape the vexations of life?

For my own part I would miss him bitterly at first, but in the army one grows used to such separations; one can count on nothing else. He made some objection at first, but I was firm, and at last we agreed that he should come no more to see me, unless there were something of importance to say to me—which would not be likely to occur.

As we sat there looking out over the lake, seeing nothing of the beauty of it, I suddenly felt him clutch my arm, and turning I saw his face wet with tears,—weak, drivelling tears, I thought,—and my heart hardened towards him; but when he burst out in a storm of grief which shook him bodily, I was moved to relent.

"You were my last friend," he said, "and you cast me off; that is what I feel, and it is bitter. But it is not a great sorrow. When I left France and when I said adieu to Algeria I did not weep; yet my grief was greater than it is now, and yet this is bitter."

"Yes," I admitted, "it is. But, you see, for me it is necessary, and you care enough for me to wish me to escape the danger of falling into your condition. If I were morally stronger it would not be needful for us to separate—but"—

"O, I know it is for the best, and we will abide by our agreement."

Slowly he stood up and said "good-night!" for the sun had gone down while we sat there, and the stars had come out. "It is 'good-by,'" I said. "Yes, good-by!"—and in the twilight he walked away, and left me sitting there. . . .

On the next evening, when De Perier did not appear at the usual time I was struck with grief. Indeed it was time I detached myself from him. But would he come? Would he break our agreement and come? Eagerly I waited and hoped; but no, he did not come. In vain I tried to read, so I got up and walked out—perhaps I would meet him. I summoned to my mind all the repugnance, all my disgust of him, but it was gone; nothing did I feel but the tenderest pity and sympathy, and the most ardent wish to see him. Up and down I walked, looking every one in the face, but De Perier did not appear. I went back sad and sorry. Why had I thrown him off? But I would see him somehow the next day, and beg him to forget what I had said; but why should I? If he had really cared for my company he would not have submitted to my request. So I continued wavering from one notion to another till a week passed. I was gradually schooling myself back to indifference and to something of my old repugnance.

But when he came running in to me one morning, my heart leaped forward to meet him.

"Halloo! what is it?" I cried.

"I've only a minute to say adieu. I'm off to Son-Tay in half an hour. I shall never see you again,—I am glad to have known you"—

"Nay, it is not 'adieu' this time either," I said. "I shall see you again, I am sure; *au revoir* till then."

He looked at me in a strange way, and his big gray eyes clouded over.

"I hope we may meet again," he said, "but it is doubtful. Good-by!" and he was gone. . . .

Shortly afterwards I left Ha-Noï to return to Yen-Luong. The boat stopped for a few minutes at Son-Tay, and of one of the soldiers loitering on the wharf I asked for news of De Perier. He did not know him, but said that if he had come lately from Ha-Noï, he was probably *en colonne*—marching after pirates.

On reaching my post I found that our company was also to start out, and all was excitement over it. We would see something of the country anyway, and if we found any pirates—why, *tant mieux—ou tant pis!*

We had been marching a long time, it seemed, when we were told of a preconcerted attack to be made on Song-Yam the next day. Two battalions of Marine Infantry were to arrive at the same point from an opposite direction. "So, then, I shall see De Perier tomorrow," I thought, and thereupon I forgot how tired I was and the mosquitoes ceased to bother me.

The attack was made; and after we had buried our dead—six was the number, I think—and cared for the wounded, we prepared to depart.

Just then a *marsouin* came into our camp asking right and left for me. "Yes? What is it? Is it De Perier?"

"How did you know? Yes, it is he, and he is dying. If you wish to see him you must come quickly."

"Ah, but I cannot go without permission; my company is to start directly, and I should be left. How has he been wounded?"

"Who said he was wounded? It's not like that, he has a fever or something. He has been out of his head for the last three hours. I supposed he was raving when he asked me to come and look for you, but it seems you know him."

"Wait a minute."

I ran to an under officer and asked permission. Yes, I could go for an hour; it would be that long before the company could start.

"Come on!" I cried; "quick! lead the way!"

In ten minutes we were in the camp of the marine infantry,

and there, lying in the shade of a clump of bamboos I found poor De Perier.

My heart sank as I saw him. Death was near, and such a death! More horrible than I had ever pictured it. All his flesh was wasted and gone; only a skeleton was left, in which was an awful, visible agony. At first he did not know me, but I knelt down and whispered in his ear. "What is it De Perier? what can I do for you?"

"Ha! it is you! see! quick! you can save me! it is all gone—you know, my opium is all gone—for four days I have had none. Oh, for the love of France find me some quick, or I am lost! O, quick! quick!"

"But how? where? O, my dear friend, if my heart were of opium I would tear it out for you, but, alas!"

Suddenly I remembered: after the attack of the day before, some of our men had pillaged in the pirates' *canias;* perchance they had found some.

"Wait," I said.

Back I ran to our camp and asked hurriedly whether any had been found, and who had it. Yes, Penhoat had found a small tin box of opium, and had sold it to a cooly for a piaster.

"Which cooly? quick!"

"That one, there, with the white rag on his arm." I had two piasters, so I ran to him.

"Donne opium mow-lemvite!" I cried. From his turban he took it, and like the wind I flew back to De Perier. No, I was not too late; he was still alive, yet the fire had died in his eyes, and he seemed calm.

"See, I have some!" I said.

Eagerly, furiously he snatched the box and pressed it to his heart.

"At last saved!—saved!" And then a new light shone across his face, and suddenly he sat up and with all his remaining strength he hurled the box of opium away from him.

"My God! De Perier, what have you done! You are dying, do you know? You have thrown your life away," and I arose to go after the opium.

"No; listen," he said, and in his voice was the ring of strength and manhood. "It is over; my agony is mortal, and why prolong it?

To-day—to-morrow, or next year; what does it matter? Here; my mother's address. Write to her; tell her—tell her—ah!" . . .

A blur came over his eyes, his voice died away, and he sank back. Over in our camp I heard the clarion sounding *"sac à dos,"* and I knew that my company was starting.

I bent over and touched De Perier's forehead with my lips. He was dead, and there I left him in the shade of the bamboos. I told his comrade whom he had sent for me, and then I rejoined my company, running for a mile before I came up with it. . . .

When we got back to Yen-Luong, I found Madame De Perier's address in one of my pockets, and I remembered what her son had said; so I wrote:

> DEAR MADAM: You will have known ere this of your son's death. I do not know what report the authorities may have made to you concerning it; but whatever you may have been told was doubtless incorrect. I, as an eye-witness, can give you a more exact account. You must know that your son died on the field of battle (*le champ d'honneur*). Many brave soldiers were killed that day, but no one died more heroically than he. By submission to the enemy he might have saved his life, but with a courage almost superhuman he preferred death to bondage; and so his death was noble—triumphant.
>
> Adieu, Madam!
>
> I have the honor to have been your son's friend, and to remain your devoted servant. . . .
>
> P.S.—His last words were of you. He bade me write to you.

THE WORST OF THE BARGAIN

The nicest native I ever met was Pho-Xa. That was the name he preferred; but to certain Catholic missionaries he had been known as Paul. He had been "Catholica" himself in those days; he had been baptized by these missionaries, and, to some extent, educated by them. But he had recanted, and had resumed his name of Pho-Xa, and his worship of the great Buddha.

Van Eycke and I were going down the river in a *chaloupe* when I saw him first. Van Eycke was a Belgian who had a knowledge of many unspeakable things, of which he was always trying to tell in untranslatable French. The reason his speech was so unusual was because at home he had heard only Wallon spoken, and nothing but Argot in the streets. The mixture of these made confusion. By the time we reached Vie-Trie I had grown weary of his talk, so all without giving offence I bade him hold his peace. At Vie-Trie a few natives came aboard, and among them was Pho-Xa. I was not observant of him at first. It was a rich family of quality which drew my attention.

There was a man with his two wives and a child, a little girl. After certain preliminary gestures of courtesy they installed themselves in a clean corner of the deck, and then they proceeded to drink *nyuk-tay* and to smoke the Annamite pipe.

The garments and jewelry of the younger woman were very fine and costly, and the inventory of them interested me. Her outer *kay-ow*, or tunic, was of sombre hue; but where it opened at the sides several others were disclosed, all of the most gorgeous colors, and each in the right relation to the others, so that none of them looked dull. Her *ka-quan* was of yellowish silk, and fell in folds over her black lacquered sandals.

Her little ears were pierced by thick links of yellow gold, and a heavy golden collar was about her neck. I had estimated all these things, and more, when my attention was averted by Van Eycke's discordant voice. He was talking to Pho-Xa, who sat staring at him as though he were an oracle of profoundest wisdom. I left off looking at the rich family, and went over to listen to Van Eycke.

"Halloo!" said he, "let me introduce you to Pho-Xa. Is that it? Isn't he nice? He can speak French. He's a school-teacher, and only eighteen years old. He"—

"All right," I interrupted; "since he knows French let him speak for himself."

Pho-Xa looked at me in surprise, wondering how I dared to snub one so wonderful as Van Eycke.

He was indeed a bright fellow, ready of understanding, and graceful of manner, with a knowledge of French which was quite unusual. I am sure that Van Eycke, whose previous life had been passed at Paris, knew nothing whatever of the inherent qualities of French verbs; but here was Pho-Xa talking about the fourth declension! O, a school-teacher indeed!

Van Eycke could not comprehend this at all, for he continued to talk to him in the jargon of common usage.

It was plain that when Van Eycke talked to me poor Pho-Xa was quite bewildered, so very few of Van Eycke's words were in his vocabulary.

Presently something in Pho-Xa's manner puzzled me: in the middle of a sentence he would hesitate and look behind in a startled way as though he were called, or as though to ward off a blow.

"What is the matter, Pho-Xa?" I asked.

"Nothing, oh, nothing,—I fear nothing!" and then after a moment, "Do you know the captain at Than-Ba?"

"You mistake," I replied; "there is no captain at Than-Ba, it is a lieutenant who has the command of that post. Yes, I know him,—why?"

"O, it is because I will teach the native *tin-yow*— the native children—at Than-Ba, and I desire that the master, the head of the post, be contented with me; that is all."

And so I went on talking with Pho-Xa, finding out several things I had long wished to know.

At least when Pho-Xa could not answer my questions he said so in French; and my ears were not vexed by the eternal "*kongo-biet.*" I saw that although Pho-Xa's garments were of rich material, they were much worn, and patched about the elbows.

He was quick to notice my scrutiny of him, and seeing perhaps a look of interest in my face he began to tell me about himself. His family, as he said, had been rich and considerable, and had dwelt at Hong-Hoa; but at the approach of French invasion the natives there had burned their houses and fled.

Pho-Xa was but a young boy then, and had been lost in the excitement and confusion of flight.

Eventually he had fallen into the hands of some French missionaries, and these had taught him more or less, and had baptized him in the Catholic religion.

"Ah," I said, "so you are Catholic?"

He looked at me sharply to see whether the truth would horrify me, but I stared vacantly at him, and then slowly he said: "No, not now; now I say, '*shim shim Buddha*,' like all my people. But my father and brother, they do not know it; they think me still 'Catholica'! My father and brother are with the pirates—they are not friends of France; they suffer much. My brother he wish to kill me; he say so; he say better I dead than Frenchman, than 'Catholica.' And so I come back to Buddha. I run away from the mission—but I find not my brother, and still he think me 'Catholica.' Now I have a word from him—one word he write to me; he write '*Thiet;*' you know: Death.

"He mean he will kill me, for that he think me Frenchman. Well, I like Frenchman too—he kind to me—

"But he not my brother! 'Catholica' not Buddha!" and Pho-Xa lapsed into silence, only to start up and look about in a scared way.

"Why don't you try to find your brother?" I asked.

"I have already sought him at all villages, but he with the pirates in the mountains. No one can tell me more of him than that. Now, I will teach in a school, I will teach the French to the little children. If France must be our mother, then we must know to speak to her—to tell her what we desire—to tell her of our sadness.

"For me it seems good that the France our mother. I read with the missionaries that she a great country, that no land before her in Europe.

"Well, we have also our civilization, our knowledge; but it can be that elsewhere in the world is more knowledge, more wisdom; it can be that French knowledge is also good. It can be that by French wisdom we find sooner Nirvannah! perhaps. The missionaries say—but you 'Catholica'; you know already what they say. Sometimes they see better than Buddha.—But they say Buddha wrong—all wrong!

"I see not that; I see wrong with Frenchman too—but not all wrong. I see."

"Fichtre! Pho-Xa; you are not wise," I said; "you must learn to shut your eyes to all such things. You must see only sunshine and the beautiful world. You must hear only harmony; when the birds sing, when the wind shakes the bamboos, when the river surges past, to these things you may listen; but when there is a noise in the clouds, when bright fire strikes across the sky, and when the missionaries dispute, then you may stop your ears; such things will make you afraid. It is better for you to learn pleasure than fear. You must begin now to find Nirvannah; but if you listen to discords you cannot reach it. Do you understand?"

"I understand a little; but there is difficulty. Do you find only pleasure and gladness? Do you hear no thunder in the sky?"

For answer I smiled somewhat grimly at Pho-Xa, and he understood.

Van Eycke had tried to follow our talk, but it seemed as nonsense to him, and he had gone away.

Then it seemed nonsense to me too, so we talked of other things till we came to Son-Tay, where Pho-Xa landed. I saw him no more for a long time, for six months or so; and then as I was sojourning at Than-Ba, Driessen, who was of that post, began to talk about Paul, the school-teacher down in the village; and he asked me to come and see him. In the evening we went down and I was presented.

"But this is not Paul! this is Pho-Xa!" I cried; and as I spoke he recognized me, and then he shook hands with me instead of with himself as he had started to do.

I glanced around the school-room and saw signs and symbols of Christianity,—crosses and crucifixes, with the Lord's Prayer printed in red.

"What is all this, Pho-Xa?" I cried. "Are you 'Catholica' again?" In a scared and deprecating way he waved his hands towards the walls, and looked at me appealingly.

"You see," he stammered, as he drew me apart from Driessen, "it is the *quan-hai;* it is the lieutenant of the post; he give me not the school; he let me not teach when I not 'Catholica.' He never let me teach *shim shim Buddha!* to *tin-yow.* All same *tin-yow* learn *shim shim Buddha!* at home, and I teach *Pater-Noster* in school. *Tin-yow* soon forget *Pater-Noster,* but not forget *shim shim Buddha!*—Come!"

And bowing with deference to Driessen, he led me back into his private chamber, where he pointed proudly to Buddha's image, where it sat smiling behind sticks of burning incense.

"So, ho!" I said. "'Catholica' in school-room and 'Buddhist' in chamber? Is that right, Paul? Is that right, Pho-Xa? Did you learn that from the missionaries, or from Buddha?"

"No, I learn it from you."

"What! From me? Are you crazy? How did you learn it from me?"

"O, you not remember? On *chaloupe* you say to me that I must find gladness. I must hear no bad things. Well, it is for me a bad thing if I have hunger, if I have no rice to eat. I cannot plant rice like *nyack-way.* I can only teach *tin-yow.* I tell you *quan-hai* send me away when I teach *shim shim Buddha!*"

"Pho-Xa, you did not tell me that the missionaries you were with were Jesuits, but I fear they must have been. I think you have taken this philosophy from them, and not from me. It is true I have told you to seek pleasure and gladness, but you will not find them in a lie. If you will be 'Catholica,' then you must forget Buddha. How can you say *Pater-Noster* and *shim shim Buddha!* at the same time?"

"Ah, but I say not *Pater-Noster* for *me;* I say him for *tin-yow.* Lieutenant say I must teach 'Catholica.' I all same as machine for *quan-hai,* so it not I who teach *Pater-Noster,* it *quan-hai.* You not see that?"

"No," I said. "I see only falsehood; if *quan-hai* know you say *shim shim Buddha* he send you away. You not see that?"

"Yes, but he not know. You not tell him?"

"No, surely I'll not tell him—but"—

But it was useless to argue: Pho-Xa had learned a little worldly wisdom, and he was putting it in practise.

It was easy to blame him, and I did blame him, but perhaps, as he said, it was indirectly my fault that he acted so; perhaps this was partly the result of what I had said to him, and so I said no more about it.

"You will still drink the tea with me?" he asked.

"O, yes; why not? I know you mean to do right, but you should not try to serve two masters. Have you not heard that from the missionaries? How can you be Buddhist and 'Catholica' at the same time?"

"Two masters?" he repeated. "Is it? Are they two masters? Are they not different pictures of the same master?

"I see so much alike in both. I am more used to Buddha's picture, and I like it better; but Christus? He too show the way to Nirvannah?—not?"—

"Pho-Xa," I said, "you must never act outwardly on such interior reasoning. You will be misunderstood,—and you will come to grief."

But Pho-Xa only smiled, and we drank the *nyuk-tay* together.

When I took leave of him I said he had better forget all I had said to him on the *chaloupe.*

And now my word was that he had best change his way of life, else, soon or late, mischief would come of it.

I predicted truer than I intended.

It was from Driessen that I learned the end of Pho-Xa's story.

A month or two after my visit to Than-Ba a pirate had been captured.

As they made ready to execute him, he said that if they would spare his life he would guide the soldiers to the stronghold in the mountains where his comrades were.

He knew that at the first sign of double-dealing on his part he would be shot, so he led the soldiers aright and betrayed his comrades.

Yet these escaped while their fortresses and *canias* were burning.

Then their betrayer was set free and led back to Than-Ba in triumph.

This was Pho-Xa's brother, and a day or two after the return the brothers met.

It seems that Pho-Xa was furious when he learned the truth, and he reviled his brother bitterly—called him a traitor who had sold his own father for the sake of his own worthless life.

Thereupon the brother began to retaliate, accusing Pho-Xa of apostasy.

By this they had reached the school-room, and there the sight of the Catholic symbols so enraged the brother that he sprang upon Pho-Xa and clove his head in twain with the large axe-like knife which he carried. There, in the morning, the *tin-yow* found their master; and seeking farther, they found the brother in the inner chamber,—dead before the shrine of Buddha.

THE PAGODA

Day after day we had been marching, and the days counted up
made weeks, and the weeks—but we lost the count. We knew,
however, that it was early in January, of 1890, when our company
started out after pirates, and we said that if we ever returned to
our post we would learn the date of our arrival, and begin again
the count of times and seasons. Now, it did not matter; one day
was just like another day, and every day unspeakably wearisome.

We had been a long time in the mountainous district of northwestern Tonquin, in the country of the Muongs. I had a map of
the land, and for a time I was able to trace our wanderings. But
eventually I lost interest in that, as well as in the course of time,
and I went blindly. As much as possible I detached my mind from
the present and lived in the past. Often there were rude awaken-
ings, as, for example, when we chanced on a few pirates, or had
unusually bad weather, but by "thinking of something else" I did
not feel the fatigue so greatly, and so I lived through it.

A great many had been unable to keep on, and our company
was losing many good soldiers. Not all of them died, for at certain
points of our march it had been possible to send the sick ones
back to post, or on to Hong-Hoa, where they could be cared for.

At length, much to my satisfaction, we left the mountains,
where marching was so hard, and where the scenery, like a
nightmare, had weighed upon me so heavily, and now we were
down in the lowlands again.

On we went, by winding streams, past green rice-fields, and
through groves of graceful palm-trees.

Sometimes we came to large villages, all deserted, with
the doors agape, and no one to bid us remain or depart. Some
villages showed signs of recent occupation, and others had been
abandoned for years.

Usually we would halt for the night or for a day's rest at one of
these hamlets, so we were seldom without a shelter.

If one can readily adapt himself to circumstances, he will suffer
much less than if he stipulate for customary usages. What, then,

did these Annamites consider a rice diet to be good? Then why should not I think so too? And it was good. Did they sleep better with a block of wood for a pillow? Ah, what dreams have I not had with my head thus at ease! Did they prefer sandals to shoes? Good again; when my shoes were worn out, a pair of sandals must serve my purpose. Thus, while many others sickened and died, I retained my health.

Sometimes we came upon the ruins of forgotten cities of unknown civilization; fragments of brick walls nearly level with the ground marked where houses had stood. Who had lived in them? Who had hated and loved and suffered here? It was ages and ages ago, and these people had been born, had grown old and died, and they never knew—never guessed, perhaps—that America existed.

They had died and left no sign except these crumbling walls, and here and there the stone image of an elephant or of some other strange animal.

Descuret, of our company, was an Egyptologist, and he was quite familiar with all that is known of the old Egyptian dynasties; so I thought I had only to appeal to him, in order to find out all I wanted to know about these ruins. But, alas! he knew his own corner of the world, and that was all. His knowledge of hieroglyphic signs was of no avail to him here; and to my amazement he was quite indifferent about it; nay, he even seemed surprised that any one could feel any interest in anything of the sort—outside of Egypt. He said, finally, that he had heard mention of certain kings called Lê, who had lived in these parts, but how, and when, and where were all unknown to him. It was useless to ask the natives. If they understood your questions or not, their answer was ever the same, "*Kongo-biet*" (I don't know), and the exasperation of it all was that no one seemed to care. What does this mean? Why do you do that? For what purpose is such a thing? Alas! no one knows. Signs and symbols of things meet one constantly; the outward form remains, but the thing signified is dead and forgotten. So these vestiges of the past ceased to interest me, and I looked at them as indifferently as did my companions.

We had wandered beyond the Black River, the *Song Bo,* and

the name of the last inhabited village we had passed was Quinh-Lam-Bao. We left it early one morning and proceeded westward. A day and part of a night we marched, and came at last to what seemed the outskirts of a village; a few scattered *canias* we found, and in them we spent the rest of the night. In the morning the coolies and native soldiers who were with us began to sniff around, and they finally concluded that these *canias* had not been very long deserted, and it was plain that Chinamen and not Annamites had been the last occupants. A speedy council was held among the officers, and it was decided to sojourn there that day, and to send out scouting parties to survey the surrounding country. We were well satisfied to have a day's rest, and forthwith we began to cook the dinner; but just then it was arranged for our squad to go over the hill to the left, and furnish two sentinels to watch in that direction.

We left the others with orders to hurry the dinner, and went off to the hill, about half a mile away. We placed one sentinel between us and the camp, and another on the brow of the hill.

The rest of us found a position in the shade, and straightway we lay down to sleep. All at once I awoke and found De Baise looking at me. "Say," he said, "there is a brook down below; let us go and wash our shirts."

"A good idea," I replied; and in a short time our shirts were drying, white and clean, on a bush. From where we sat waiting we could see a large *cania*, and De Baise suggested that we should go and look inside; we might find something.

"All right," I said; "but go and get your rifle first, for we may find more than we wish."

In a few minutes he had fetched it, and cautiously we proceeded to examine the *cania*. We found much rice and paddy in separate bins, and along one wall were hens' nests in a row, containing many fresh eggs.

"Good!" I cried, "we need not care now whether they send us our dinner or not."

While De Baise began to fill a basket I climbed up a ladder into the upper chamber, where I found a series of big black lacquered boxes, all filled with books—Chinese books which no one could read. The place was dark and mouldy, so I pushed open a side of the wall and propped it up like an awning. In doing this I saw the red-tiled roof of a pagoda farther down the hill. It was half hidden by the branches of a banyan-tree, but I saw that the corners of the roof were tilted up, and this assured me that it was a pagoda, and not another *cania*.

I called De Baise up, but all he said was: "Fusty old books! Come on back. I'm going to make an omelet."

"You can make *au rhum*," I said, "or *au tschum-tschum* rather. There is a jar of it in the corner."

He made one spring, and had his nose at the jar directly.

"Hooray!" he shouted, "so it is! You take the eggs, and come along."

"Hold on! you forget your shirt," I cried, for he was making rapid strides up to the squad. In a few minutes we were back, and I was just in time to relieve one of the sentinels; De Baise should have relieved the other, but he wanted to cook the eggs, so he changed places with Descuret.

"Wait a little," he said; "don't you want a drink of *tschum-tschum* before you go?" and he proceeded to pour out for us. It was not the ordinary distillation of rice, but a particular sort, known as *ton-doc*, strong and sweet, with a smack of orange peel.

It was Geniets whom I relieved, and as he went I told him to keep his eye on De Baise.

"He's got a jar of *tschum-tschum*," I said, "and he'll have you all drunk before midday, unless you are prudent."—"*Tschum-tschum?* Where did he get it?" But without waiting to hear he was off for his share of it.

Looking about me in all directions I observed the sprawling limbs of a banyan-tree, and then I remembered the pagoda, the roof of which I had seen from the *cania*. I had not spoken of it to De Baise, because his excitement over the *tschum-tschum* had put it out of my head.

During the first part of my sentry duty I felt fresh and exhilarated. A clean shirt and a cup of *tschum-tschum* had made a change in my spirits, so that I saw the bright side of everything— even of this interminable march. But soon the sun reached the zenith, and my enthusiasm all trickled away in perspiration. I was sure my two hours were finished long ago, yet no one came to relieve me. Faintly I could hear the murmur of voices up at the squad, and, yes, that was De Baise singing in a weak falsetto:

"N'allez pas chez le marchand de vin, qui fait le coin, coin, coin!"

"Yes," I thought, "they are all drunk, and the corporal too; and here I may stand till I drop,—the mean pigs!"

But by and by Van Eycke came jogging along to take my place (the corporal had not bothered to come with him), and as I saw he was quite well able to stand up, I gave him the watchword, and went back to the squad. De Baise had gone to relieve Descuret, but he had left me a big slab of burned omelet reeking of *tschum-tschum*. However, the soup had come from the camp, so I did not grumble. After an hour's sleep I sat up with my thoughts running on the pagoda.

"Is there any of the *tschum-tschum* left?" asked Descuret, who also was awake.

"I don't know," I said, "look in the jar; it's there by the tree."

There was a little, and we shared it.

"Where did you get it?" he asked.

"Down there in a *cania*. I say, will you come and examine a pagoda that is just beyond? Take your rifle and come."

"Hadn't we better tell the corporal?" he asked.

"You can, if you like; but he's asleep, and he'll not thank you for waking him."

"Come on, then," he said; "where is it?"

"Not far; that banyan-tree down there hides it; we'll be there in a minute."

"If you think we can find any more *tschum-tschum*?" he whispered.

"What? In a pagoda? Are you crazy?"

"No, of course not, but you said there was a *cania*."

"Yes, yes, there's the *cania*, over there, but De Baise and I were all through it, and found only one jar; you can go in and look, if you like, and I'll mount guard. You'll see the roof of the pagoda from the upper chamber. Hurry up!"

In a little while he came out, carrying a dead chicken.

"We'll roast this for our supper," he said.

"But look here; I saw the roof of your pagoda, and I don't want to see any more of it. Come on back." And in a hesitating way he began to pluck at the chicken.

"Why; what's the matter with you now? Why don't you want to go?"

"Because this is Friday—my unlucky day."

"Ho! ho!" I jeered. "This from you! But how in the world do you know it's Friday? Have you found a calendar in the *cania*? Ten to one it's Sunday! Come on, don't be a fool! What would your friend Geniets say if I were to tell him this? How did you make the discovery that to-day is Friday?"

"How do I know that fire will burn me? I know it's Friday because I feel it. I feel there is misfortune in the air. Can't you feel it?"

By this he had the leg of the fowl all plucked bare, and as sober as a sphinx he began at the other.

"See here, Descuret," I snapped out, "you disgust me: you throw scorn at these poor natives on account of their superstitions; they burn sticks and paper, and scatter rice and salt, all to ward off evil influences. Suppose you go back and get a handful of rice and try it; you'll find some in the left-hand corner,—you and your Fridays! Once for all, are you coming?"

He looked up from his chicken and said: "Yes, since you are so bent upon it."

"Leave your chicken here, then; we'll come back this way—and hurry up!" He placed the half-plucked fowl behind a clump of ferns, and we went on. At the foot of the hill we found "a sudden little river" supplied from a stream higher up. We walked along the bank, but found no place to ford. We could see the high white wall enclosing the pagoda at about a stone's throw from where we stood debating.

"Look!" I said; "there's a bridge farther down." Sure enough; and in a few minutes we were at the walls looking for an entrance. On the south side we found a gate flanked by two plastered pillars, crowned by furious griffins with porcelain eyeballs, glittering fearfully. The gate was of some heavy wood, and it resisted our efforts to push it in.

"Wait a minute," I said; "give me a hand to get over the wall, and I'll open it from the inside and let you in."

A branch of the banyan-tree came within my reach, and by a little effort I pulled myself up and got over. As I dropped into the court-yard a chill shuddered through me, but not waiting to analyze it, I ran and unbarred the gate, and let Descuret in. The countless trunks of the tree filled the place, and its branches and serpentine roots were like the tentacles of some gigantic polypus with the pagoda in their clutches.

Strange plants grew in the corners of the yard, and parasitic ferns and lichens were everywhere suspended. The whole place was dank and dark, and curiously like a picture out of Dante's "Inferno." I shuddered again as we stood there hesitating.

The walls on the interior were covered with bas-reliefs of elephants, and with colossal storks standing on the backs of enormous turtles; then there were drawings in black and white of birds, of impossible flowers, and of men—Chinamen—in improbable postures. All this was Chinese art—original or copied.

In front of us was the pagoda on a higher level, with broad low steps leading to it. The tiled roof with its great carved rafters was supported by vast wooden pillars, based on large flat stones.

Three monstrous wooden statues of Buddha, sitting in a row, faced the entrance. These were painted and gilded and lacquered, in radiant brightness, as contrasted with the gloom of their surroundings. They were raised a few feet above the floor, and while the two end ones looked stern and forbidding, the one between them smiled invitingly. On approaching, we found these statues to be of superior workmanship, and not like the ordinary images we were used to.

On a low table before each of them were placed the usual offerings of paper horses, paper shoes, bundles of paper cubes; and what were these? bars of gold and silver? No; they were only little pieces of wood skilfully covered with tinsel. The intention was magnanimous, and Buddha probably winked at the deception.

"Well, have you seen enough?" asked Descuret. "There is nothing new; we may as well go back. It's the same old story that we've seen a hundred times."

"What, you're not afraid, are you? Let us go in, and we may find some pieces of bronze, some small image of Buddha. Ziegledach found one in a pagoda at Daï-Lisch, and sold it to the administrator for ten piasters. Let us look, as long as we are here."

We walked in, past the three images, and found a series of altars with numbers of other smaller images smiling blandly at us from all sides. There were tall, wooden screens standing about, some of them miraculously carved, and others strangely incrusted with mother-of-pearl.

In looking about I began to feel uneasy in my mind. I had been poking and peering here and there for any portable object of art, with the innocent intention of appropriating it in the face of all the gods, but something checked me, and I plucked at Descuret, and said: "Come, then, if you want to, I've seen enough. As you say, there is nothing new here." But he had been set on fire by what I had said about Ziegledach finding the small bronze Buddha, and was as eager to stay as at first he had been eager to go.

"Hold on," he said; "look up there!" and he pointed to the carved cross-beams of the roof, on which was placed a long coffin-shaped box.

"O, that is nothing," I said; "I know what's in that. It is where they always keep the big paper umbrellas, wooden axes, swords, and spears, *et cetera;* all the old paraphernalia of a religious service. You've seen it all scores of times."

"Well, and what if I should find a small bronze Buddha there too? What would you say to that? Wait. I'm going up."

"Well, make haste," I said, for my feeling of uneasiness was increasing.

Glancing around the enclosure it seemed as if all the images had fixed me with their gleaming eyes; and I was anxious to get out into the sunlight again, away from the place.

"Hurry up! hurry up! I'm getting the fever," I cried, for I felt cold thrills coursing up and down my spine. I helped him drag over a heavy wooden ladder-like stair, and I watched him as he mounted to the box up on the cross-beams.

A certain feeling of safety while he stood near me had kept back my fear, but now that I stood alone I began to tremble. No, it was not the fever which was in my blood, but fear—actual terror. I wanted to call out to him and bid him to come back, but, as if I were in a nightmare, I could not open my lips.

Letting my glance fall from him, as catlike he was working out on a broad beam towards the box, my eyes met those of an image, not noticed till then. Its face was like a hideous Japanese mask, and it leered at me in a mad, mocking way, ghastly and horrible.

Again I tried to cry out, but my voice died in my throat; and an instant's thought told me it was well it had done so, for how easily might I have startled Descuret and made him fall.

I looked up to him again and saw he had reached the box and had opened it; he was kneeling beside it, poking in it with his right hand.

A strange sweet odor came down and filled the whole pagoda. 'Twas like the souls of all the roses that had ever bloomed.

> "And strew faint sweetness from some old
> Egyptian's fine, worm-eaten shroud
> Which breaks to dust when once unrolled."

Vaguely these lines of Browning's came into my mind, and for the nonce my fear was gone.

But, good God! what was that in Descuret's face? As I stood gazing at him a look of unspeakable terror struck across it, and from his blanched lips an awful cry escaped. Then back—he struggled back—recoiling from the accursed box, and came falling headlong to the floor. My own fear was at its climax, and echoing his scream I darted forward to save him from death. He crushed me down with him, but in an instant he bounded to his feet, and I staggered to mine, and out we ran, as though ten thousand devils were after us. We never stopped till we reached the squad, where the corporal was still asleep, and where De Baise, back from his two hours' duty, sat nibbling a piece of leather-like omelet.

As we came rushing up with wild fear in our eyes he jumped to his feet and said: "What is it? Pirates? Where are they? Are they coming?"

I shook my head. "No, it's not pirates; I—I don't know what it is—we—I—ask him!" I stammered, pointing to Descuret.

But Descuret threw himself down on the ground and hid his face in his hands; he lay there breathing heavily and trembling in every muscle.

The corporal awoke and said: "He's got the fever; two of you lead him back to the camp, and get him some quinine. Tell the captain." Then he looked at me and asked: "Have you got the fever too?"

"No," I replied; "I'll be all right presently. I'm frightened, that's all."

Geniets came up then, and seeing his friend Descuret lying there shaking, he stooped and asked him what was the matter.

"We were in a pagoda down there," I explained, "and he climbed up to look in a box. I don't know what he saw in it, but he was frightened and fell backwards to the floor. He is bruised, I guess." And then I realized that my own right wrist was sprained so that I could not bend it: it was all swollen. "See," I cried, "he fell on me. Ask him what he saw." And Geniets, with his voice at Descuret's ear and his hand on his shoulder, whispered: "What is it, old chap? What did you see in the box?"

But Descuret only shuddered and shrunk closer to the ground. Soon he turned over and sat up, and then it was plain that his fear had been great, for part of his hair had turned white.

"IT moved!" he gasped. "IT moved when I touched IT; a long yellow hand, with long finger-nails; IT clutched at my hand as I groped in the box."

"Where? What box?" asked the corporal, who was listening.

But just then an under officer from the camp arrived with the order that we should all return, and get ready to march within the hour. Descuret struggled to his feet and said: "It is time we got away from this damned place! Come on,—but where's my rifle?" At the same instant I realized that my rifle too was missing!

"Good heavens!" I cried. "We left our rifles at the gate of the pagoda, and did not stop for them as we ran out; we'll have to go back for them."

"Never!" screamed Descuret. "I'll not go back for anything; but Geniets will go with you,—and (with his teeth still chattering)— and get the chicken when you're coming back; it's behind a clump of ferns near the *cania*."

APPENDIX

The Great Buddha

Since the French have invaded Tonquin there have been many changes effected in Ha-Noï, which is the chief city of that strange country. At present the Annamites seem reconciled to their new masters, and apparently they regard the advance of European civilisation with resignation if not with favour. In the Rue Paul Bert—(named after the devoted Governor-General, whose best policy was conciliation)—there are lofty French-roofed houses, which look down in wonder, and a little scorn, on the few pagoda-like shops and dwellings, with their curious decorations and turned-up cornices, which have not yet been crowded away. There are side-walks, too—wide asphalte side-walks—in the Rue Paul Bert, but the native population still walk in the middle of the street, for the traffic is not yet so thriving as to make that dangerous.

There is a pretty lake near the French quarter of Ha-Noï, which is surrounded by grassy banks and fine flower-gardens, wherein roses bloom from year's end to year's end. From the middle of the lake rises a big stone pedestal, surmounted by a modified statue of "Liberty lighting the world." Then, at the north end of the lake, is a little island on which grows a great clump of bamboo-trees, and, half-hidden by them, is an old pagoda with moss-covered roof and crumbling grey walls; and there is a pretty pavilion, with stone steps which lead down to the water's edge; in the background stands a tall tower, with red "tip-tilted" roof, very picturesque and graceful. But in all the rest of Ha-Noï there are very few attractive features; all the land is flat and changeless, as far as the eye can see; perhaps, though, if the city could be seen from a height, it might present a fairer picture.

At the north-west end of Ha-Noï lies an immense citadel, in which the French have four or five military barracks, and in which several old Chinese palaces and pagodas still remain. An arched gateway, near what used to be the palace of a great mandarin, is exceedingly beautiful; evidently it inspired the French, for they have built another gateway opposite, which serves, indeed, as a clock-tower; but though they have tried to copy the original, the result is but a foolish caricature.

Several times I started out to walk around the outside of the citadel, a distance of several miles, but I never accomplished it, because, as soon as I had gone a quarter of the way, I was always drawn on to another road—the road which led to the "Pagoda of the Great Buddha."

Although I had often visited this pagoda, it never ceased to interest me; it was almost in spite of myself that whenever I was in the neighbourhood I went in to see again the great image of Buddha, and the other objects of Oriental art there enclosed. The gateway through which the courtyard is entered is even more elaborately decorated than the pagoda itself; over the arch of it is a watchtower, or *mirador,* from which one may see over the roof of the pagoda, and far off in all directions; a balcony, with a beautiful balustrade, goes all around this watch-tower, and stone stairways descend from it at the sides. Frequently in Chinese architecture the peculiarity of the details almost spoil, in our eyes, the proportions of the whole; but the gateway with its *mirador* is an exception, since seen from any side it is most admirable. Outside, in front of the gateway, are two high, square columns, crowned, not as is usual with grinning dragons, but with floriated capitals exquisitely sculptured. Having passed in at the gateway, you find yourself in a cleanly-swept courtyard enclosed by high walls. Many strange plants grow in the corners, and at one side a gigantic banyan-tree throws its great branches and dangling roots far and wide; large tufts of parasitic ferns and many creeping plants hide the bareness of its sprawling limbs.

In the wall facing the gateway a large opening leads into a second courtyard; it is flanked by bas-reliefs of elephants with natural tusks protruding. On the side-wall are drawings, in black and white, of Chinese landscapes, &c., done in that surprising reality of style of which Chinese artists best know the secret. In the second courtyard stands the pagoda, a wide building with low-reaching eaves, the corners of which are tilted up several feet, and finished in writhing serpents. Two columns, of lesser proportions than the ones outside, stand one at each corner of the pagoda, and glaring and grinning from their tops are stone dragons of frightful aspect. Broad stone steps, the whole width of the pagoda, lead up to the entrance. There is a series of narrow folding doors to shut the entrance, and these, with their jambs and architraves and transoms, are all carved and sculptured in a way which European wood-carvers would wonder at—and they would wonder still more if they were to see the two or three simple carving-tools with which in China and other Eastern countries these wonderful carvings are executed. Inside of the pagoda, a few steps from the doors, is an altar of black wood, lacquered, and inlaid with mother-of-pearl in arabesques and strange designs; placed at the back of it are two huge bouquets of wonderfully-shaped flowers and leaves, made of gold and silver tinsel and coloured paper. In the centre of the altar stands a large brown vase of earthenware, enamelled on the outside; it is filled with sand, in which are sticking long splinters of bamboo wood, covered with a black hard paste of incense, and as they slowly burn they give forth a pleasant odour to the place.

At each end of this altar—if it may be called an altar—is placed the image of a stork standing on a turtle's back; but though this symbol is so frequently seen in pagodas I have never been able to learn exactly what it signifies. But here you are in the pagoda; yet so far nothing is seen of "the Great Buddha," which pilgrims and tourists come so far to see, to pray to, or to wonder at. It is Nam-Si who must show us this great bronze image. But I speak too fast. Nam-Si is dead, and his functions are now performed by another; by whom I do not know, for after Nam-Si's death I never saw the place again.

When I first saw Nam-Si he was already old, and his features were covered by a network of wrinkles. From his almond-shaped eyes and certain other indications, it was evident that certain of his ancestors had been Chinese, though, perhaps, he never suspected it himself. His long grey hair, which reached to his knees when it was unwound, was always worn in the Annamite fashion, and his garments were such as were worn by Annamites of the better class. His long black silk *ca-ow* (tunic) was darned and patched at the cuffs and elbows; and instead of being made of white silk, his *ca-quan* (trowsers) was of course white calico; his *ba-ba* (turban) was also of white calico, but that was in sign of mourning, or rather in sign of his widowhood, for he had been married and his wife had been dead many years. The turban usually worn by well-to-do Annamites is of dark purple crape-like silk.

In spite of his wrinkles and his poverty, I saw in his narrow twinkling eyes, and in his quiet, humble bearing, signs of an innocent simplicity and gentleness, which attracted me and led me to inquire about him. The jumble of French and Annamite words, which alone I was able to exchange with himself, served rather to confuse than to enlighten me about his past. Another thing which distinguished him from his neighbours was that his teeth were white and natural, and not covered with the black enamel which, as a rule (to enhance their beauty!), all Annamites have applied to their teeth; and neither were his lips stained red by the everlasting chewing of betel. Nam-Si lived on charity. All the pious pilgrims and curious sight-seers who visited his pagoda always gave him an alms. Almsgiving is the great virtue of the Buddhists, and importunate alms-begging is a quality in which Annamite children are very proficient; and this is indeed the disagreeable thing about visiting the Great Buddha, for no sooner does one come near, than a cloud of ragged children, carrying their younger brothers or sisters astride their hips, flocks up, piping out the shrill chorus, *Donne tin-yow sou! donne tin-yow sapek!* ("Give the little one a cent! give the little one a sapeck!") Even to the doors of the pagoda will they pursue you; but there you will be met by Nam-Si—I mean his successor—who will drive them back, and shake hands with himself, and bow low to salute you.

After you have examined the altar, and the storks, and the tinsel flowers, and a richly embroidered reredos, he will light a taper and conduct you down a dark passage on the left side of the pagoda. It is bordered by great round wooden pillars, and leads into a chamber behind the altar, but all is hidden in thick darkness. By-

and-by, as you wait, the pale light of the taper will spread through the place, and reveal, one by one, strange unfamiliar objects.

On my first visit I was profoundly impressed by it all. It was not exactly fear that I felt, and yet the sensation of a similar indefinable feeling checked my curiosity and made me hesitate. The presence of certain persons is so real, so intense, that though we may not be able to see them, we can *feel* that they are in the same room with us. So it was as I waited there. I felt a presence other than that of Nam-Si—an indistinct but palpable presence of the unknown and the unknowable; and I think I would have had a very distinct fear if Nam-Si had not been there with his light. Gradually I became aware of something like a vast yellow pyramid reaching up higher than the light, and I saw it was the form of something covered with a yellow cloak of silk damask—yellow?— and I remembered then of having read somewhere that Buddha, or namely Fo, or Xaca, or Sakya-mouni, as he was diversely called in China, Japan, and India, chose the yellow dress because, hundreds of years before our era, the poorest and vilest class or caste in India dressed in yellow. What, then, was this the image of Buddha, this great pyramid which rose up twenty, thirty feet, up to the roof of the pagoda? Yes. . . . Very reverently Nam-Si drew back the cloak, and gave me the taper to hold that I might the better examine it. Yes, of dark, gleaming bronze, it was a statue of Buddha in a sitting posture; his right hand held up as if in blessing, or was it in warning? In his left hand was a sword with a dragon twisting around it, but it was not raised; it was pointed downward. I clambered over his right foot and threw the light up into his face. I had expected to be disappointed, for images of Buddha and other immortals found in pagodas very often lack expression, and are nothing but images. This was something more. The artist who had modelled it had put life into it, and yet not human life either. I do not know what it was, or how to explain it; but it seemed somehow as if this image would speak to me if only I could hear and understand; such was my impression. The ears, it is true, were inordinately long, but that indicated genius; the nose was flat and the mouth large, and the eyes narrow and oblique;

but in the *ensemble* there was a strange dignity—a placid calmness, and I thought: "Surely, one who had found *Nirvana* would look like that, when all earthly hopes, and fears, and longings, and strivings were over; when all human passions had passed away, such would be the expression in the face."

For a long time I gazed in wonder and admiration, believing, indeed, that there were more things in heaven and earth than were dreamed of in my philosophy. Carefully and gently Nam-Si drew the yellow cloak together again, and I turned to examine the rest of the chamber. All at once I started back, for on the left side of the Great Buddha was a bonze writing at a small table. Was *his*, then, the presence which I had felt in the place? No; for this too was but an image—an image of stone, but painted and carved in a style so lifelike and natural, that I was positive for a minute that it was a living human being—the shaven head, the dark-greenish yellow face, from which the beard was plucked out, the slender Asiatic hands with prehensile fingers, and finger-nails two inches long, all was startlingly realistic. He, too, was dressed in yellow, for the bonzes or priests of Buddha have followed Buddha's example in this. There were two or three other images in the chamber, but I looked in vain for the three black Africans, and for the woman surrounded by small figures representing the human passions, and for some other immortals which are always enthroned in ordinary pagodas. They were not there, neither was there trace of any of Brahma's various incarnations. Buddha was all supreme.

As we turned to leave the chamber Nam-Si stopped to make his *shim-shim* (salutation) to Buddha, and from his attitude and reverent manner I saw a little how he loved and honoured this great image of his divinity.

In the year 1888 there had been some talk among the French of taking *le Grand Bouddha* to the Exposition of 1889 at Paris, and I learned that Nam-Si had then been in such a state of fear and excitement, that his neighbours thought he was out of his mind. He ran from the *Ton-doc* to the *Quan-fou*, from one Annamite dignitary to another, till he had inspired them with some of his own ardour and resentment. What then? The French, not satisfied with having taken the country, must also try to take away its gods. Oh, but no! that should not be; and so the plan had to be abandoned. Perhaps it was never seriously entered upon; although elephants are often transported from one country to another, and although machinery has been made by means of which Egyptian obelisks have been taken, one to France, one to England, and even one to America, yet some exceptional means would be needed in order to take the Great Buddha to Paris. But Nam-Si imagined that his efforts alone had saved it, and so he rejoiced.

On coming out of the pagoda there were the clamorous children waiting for me; but Nam-Si frightened them away, and as they scampered out of the courtyard a magnificent peacock flew up and alighted on the balustrade of the *mirador*, where the sunlight shone upon his gorgeous plumage and made a splendour beautiful to see.

Very humbly Nam-Si drew me aside towards his lodging, and begged of me to take tea with him—such bad tea from such a beautiful cup! Still I drank it; what could one not drink from such a cup! The teapot, kept warm in a padded basket, was likewise an exquisite example of ceramic art. But somehow my mind was so full of the Great Buddha that I had no eyes for tea-cups, though they were never so fine. Nay; it was only on my third visit that I noticed the details of Nam-Si's lodge. In an alcove was his bed, that is, if a wooden table six feet square, raised two feet from the ground, covered with a straw mat, and having an oblong block of wood for a pillow, could indeed be called a bed. Over it was a coloured picture of Buddha with religious signs and symbols surrounding it; and under it, on a shelf, were Nam-Si's poor *Penates*, as I supposed. Conversation with Nam-Si was unsatisfactory and difficult. When I should have said *faï* (yes), I said *kong* (no); and when he should have said *non*, he said *oui*; but all the same, we were able to read a little in each other's mind and meaning, and we liked each other none the less for our blundering tongues. Sympathy and good-will never need to be translated into words; the deaf and the dumb can evince and recognise them as accurately as the polyglot whose hearing is perfect.

I have often wondered how it is that these Orientals, whose voices, when they speak, are always so soft and harmonious, have such bizarre ideas of music. I listened a few times to Nam- Si's singing; what it was about I could not guess, but the tune he sang—always the same—was very peculiar; it was all on three notes; one note a very high flat; another very low, but natural, with the burden of the song on a middle note somewhat sharpened. Frequently I have heard coolies singing together in this manner; but as some of them would soar to the high note, while others kept on the low note, and still others were struggling along in the middle, the effect was very astonishing. Sometimes Nam-Si accompanied his singing on a sort of a single-stringed harp, and though the result was strange and barbarous, it still had a weird sort of charm. Once, as I heard the name of Buddha often repeated in a song he was singing, I concluded that it was of a religious character; and, on questioning him, I gathered that it was a song of gladness or triumph which he had made about the success of his efforts in saving the Great Buddha from being taken away by the *Ton-doc Lang-sa* (governor from far away).

"O, Buddha, whom I now salute in humility, thou knowest that I love thee, and that from the eyes of strangers who ignore thy greatness, and smile scornfully on thy servants, I have kept and guarded thine image, so sublimely majestic. O Buddha, again I salute thee! *Shim-shim Buddha! Shim-shim Buddha!*"

One morning as I was walking through one of the busy streets, near the Chinese quarter of Ha-Noï, I met an Annamite funeral procession. Three or four young men walked before the bier, carrying aloft standards whereon were perpendicular rows of inscriptions in Annamite characters. The bier, fantastically decorated with tinselled forms and embroidered hangings, was carried on trestles which lifted it up above the heads of the bearers. Walking under it, with bowed heads, were four *kongoïs* (native women) dressed in white, which is the colour of mourning; over all they wore tunics of loosely woven bamboo fibres, each fibre half an inch apart; and down their backs their long black hair was hanging to the ground. As they slowly moved along under the bier, they wailed out a dolorous litany, which sounded hopeless and melancholy. After the bier came a group of musicians playing on strange instruments; then came more standard-bearers, then a sort of a shrine grotesquely ornamented, then more chanting women, more musicians, more standard-bearers, and all followed by a group of natives—men, women, and children. I asked a passer-by if he knew whose funeral it was, and I heard with surprise and regret that it was Nam-Si who was being transported to his grave. I would gladly have followed the convoy, but I was even then making ready to leave Ha-Noï; so it was that I saw no more of Nam-Si, nor of the Great Buddha which he had so jealously guarded during his lifetime. All that is earthly of Nam-Si lies buried in an uncultivated rice-field, which is bordered by lofty bamboo-trees; over his grave they cast flickering shadows till the sun be high in the heavens; all day long they rustle their pointed leaves, whispering secretly about Nam-Si, the friend of Buddha, who lies buried below; not Nam-Si himself, however; he, that is the soul of him, the germ, the essence, has now passed into another form, and, because of his past virtues, into a higher being. In a year or two, when the rice-field may be ploughed and planted again, no trace will remain of Nam-Si's grave; but why should there be, since he is not there—since even his earthly remains have disintegrated and passed away, have entered into other forms, graceful forms of green leaves and waving grasses?

Good Words 35 (1894): 851–55.

Maurus Jókai

Whenever I hear the name Hungarian, my German jacket
becomes too small for me."—HEINE

To the American public Maurus Jókai is little known; to book-han-
dlers, perhaps, to certain philomaths, and to some novel-readers;
but even for these his name is not one to conjure with. I am afraid
that we know very little of Magyar literature—perhaps because
the Magyar language is so difficult. But these Hungarians learn
English, it seems, and all of our writers of any note are very well
known to them. In order to rank with the foremost nations of
the world, Hungary has neglected no means by which she might
advance. Seeing that the Anglo-Saxons were leading the race, she
has fixed her eyes on us and drawn inferences and inspirations.
Perhaps now, if we would glance back at her, we might profit a
little by what she can show.

Maurus Jókai was born on 18 November 1825; so he has
already reached three score and ten, which is the age of man. Yet
his labor is not ended; he has undertaken another work, which
cannot be completed within four or five years to come. This will
be the climax (or the anti-climax?) of his whole work. For fifty
years he has been writing romances; and the number of them
is fabulous: three hundred and fifty volumes—seven volumes a
year! And the number of his poems, pamphlets, essays, etc. (not
counted with these volumes), is past reckoning! All this from one
man; all produced without secretary or amanuensis; everything
corrected, noted and indexed by his own hand. This is astonishing, is it not?

But to go back. His father, Joseph Jókay, Elder of Asva, was a
nobleman. The letter *y* instead of *i* at the end of his name was,
in his day, the sign and privilege of nobility. Maurus, also, spelled
his name with a *y* till the revolution of 1848, and then he had to
change it for the *i*. He was what the Germans call a *Tauschkind*—
that is, a changeling—I don't know how else to translate the word;

but this was the way of it: German and Hungarian families had, seventy years ago, the "beautiful custom" of interchanging their children during the first years of infancy—a boy for a boy and a girl for a girl, so that these might the better learn the two languages. Thus Jókai, in his early childhood, lived with a German family at Presburg. Poesy and painting were the "noble passions" of his youth, only, as they brought little except pleasure and honor, it was thought expedient for him to study law as well, even as his father had done. Still, literature attracted him; and when he found a Hungarian translation of "Ivanhoe," he read it with enthusiasm. Then came "Pickwick," "The Last of the Mohicans" and "Bug-Jargal"; and later on the romances of Eugène Sue. These roused his admiration considerably, but when he read "King Lear" and "Richard III," he knew no rest by day or night. With Petöfi, who was before the public at that time as an actor, he learned English and French, without a master, and together they translated "King Lear" and had it performed on the Kecskemet stage. The result was most flattering; the theatre was filled with an enthusiastic audience, which "went wild" over the genius of the world's poet.

Then Jókai composed a drama himself, to which was awarded a prize of one hundred ducats by the Academy. This was the beginning of his literary career; but all this time he was studying law, and, having passed his examinations, was called to the bar. He did not go, however, for literature had become his true vocation. At the age of twenty-one he became the editor of a liberal journal, devoted rather to art than to politics. Then came the year 1848, when politics put an end to literature. During the trouble and excitement of that time, Jókai made the acquaintance of Rosa Laborfalvy, the greatest actress on the Hungarian stage; she had played "Adrienne Lecouvreur" in the presence of Rachel, and "Lady Macbeth" along with Aldridge. Jókai fell in love with her, and they were married. He had taken an active part in the revolution, so, when the reaction came, he was proscribed and eventually sentenced to death as a dangerous firebrand. He escaped, however, and, while he was in hiding, his wife obtained provisional pardon for him. For some years his name was not heard, yet his pen was still active; he wrote under the pseudonym of "Sajo"—a name usually applied to dogs.

And now the style of his writing began to change. Phantasy and bombast disappeared, and reality and earnestness succeeded. Was this in the air, or had he perhaps heard tell of the pre-Raphaelite movement in England, which had its birth at the same time? Whichever way it was, *Naturam sequere* became his maxim, and when he heard how a peasant woman had said, while reading one of his tales, "I could write like that myself," he saw that he was on the right road. Greater works were now undertaken. "The Hungarian Nabob" and "Zoltan Karpáthy" were two important novels. Then came the Hungarian "Decamerone": a hundred tales in brilliant coloring. Nor was the drama neglected. "Dalma," "George Dosza" and the "Martyrs of Szegetvar" followed each other in quick succession. Again he became the editor of a journal, in which he proposed that Hungarians should dress in national costume rather than according to the caprice of fashion. This was adopted throughout the country, and many signs of it are still visible.

Jókai has often been accused—with some justice, I think—of traveling too far in the region of fancy; but he repels the charge, and says that judgment and memory, as well as fancy, have been his watchwords; he says that where his fancy seems to soar highest, there may be most reality. We know very well that "truth is stranger than fiction," and so fiction should be careful not to sail too near the truth, when it becomes so "passing strange." Indeed, during the half-century of his literary career, Jókai has seen strange sights and heard strange things; and it is not to be wondered at if they have got into his books. He never disdained hints; here a word from one, there a tale from another; all was grist that came to his mill; and from the rough uncouth material he produced beautiful results. All sorts of knowledge are useful to him, and the reading of the daily press must not be neglected. Five languages he knows, and can find his way in three or four others. National history and natural history are familiar to him, and I know not what of the exact sciences.

Jókai lives in the characters he creates—he feels all the horror of being a villain, a murderer, an atheist; and one wonders how his nervous system has stood fifty years of this sort of thing. His present book, on which he has been at work for some years, is a Hungarian "Nibelungen Lied." History and tradition are to be mixed in it; now told in poesy and anon in prose; no new word, no new thought, for this is the past; and all shall be told in simplicity and clearness, so that he who runs may read; yet the whole work will embody a great ethical and political idea. When this is ended as he desires, Jókai will lay down his pen.

The Critic 31 (November 6, 1897): 261.